T0078265

CAPTAIN
PROTON™

STAR TREK: VOYAGER®PRESENTS

CAPTAIN
PROTON™

DEFENDER OF THE EARTH

By D.W. "Prof" Smith

Pocket Books

NEW YORK LONDON TORONTO SYDNEY SINGAPORE

An *Original* Publication of POCKET BOOKS

POCKET BOOKS, a division of Simon & Schuster Inc.
1230 Avenue of the Americas, New York, NY 10020

STAR TREK is a Registered Trademark of Paramount Pictures.

This book is published by Pocket Books, a division of Simon and Schuster Inc., under exclusive license from Paramount Pictures.

ISBN: 0-671-03646-7

First Pocket Books printing November 1999

10 9 8 7 6 5 4 3 2 1

POCKET and colophon are registered trademarks of Simon & Schuster Inc.

Cover lettering by Jim Lebbad
Cover art by David McMacken/Bernstein & Andriulli, Inc.

Printed in the U.S.A.

DEFENDER OF THE EARTH

VOL.9, NO.7   CONTENTS   FALL ISSUE

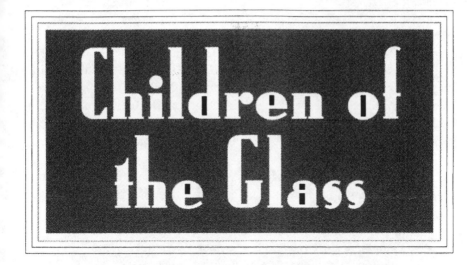

A Full-Length

CAPTAIN PROTON

Novel

By D. W. "Prof" Smith

CHAPTER 1: A DOOR OPENS

The Interspacial Cross-Galactic Door opened about two feet behind Constance Goodheart's chair as she leaned forward to daintily sip her soup, a chicken bisque flavored with the thick richness of the Jovian Emir plant. The Door opened with a faint sucking sound, as if Constance had made a rude noise with her soup, which she never would have done. In all the years Constance had been Captain Proton's secretary, he had never heard her make a rude noise. Lots of screams, but never, ever rude noises. That type of thing was just not in her nature.

With a second rude noise, the Interspacial Cross-Galactic Door shimmered, then stabilized just above the carpet, covering everything with a faint blue tinge.

Captain Proton had reserved the private dining room of the Moon's most famous restaurant, Tranquillity Fine Dining, just for the occasion of having a nice, quiet dinner with his secretary, Constance Goodheart. With so much going on around the galaxy, with so many problems, it had been a long time since they had had a dinner together when they could just sit and talk. Both Captain Proton and Constance had been looking forward to the evening and the wonderful food always served by Chef Henry of Tranquillity.

Now it was ruined!

"Move!" Captain Proton shouted at Constance as the rude noise made him look up and he saw the door. He instantly recognized it for an Interspacial Door from the shape and the blue tint of everything close by. Such doors were very expensive to operate, took massive amounts of power, and were illegal on every world in the Incorporated Planets.

But Captain Proton had learned that something being illegal never stopped the bad elements of the Galaxy.

Constance looked up at Captain Proton over her soup, a small drop of the bisque glistening on her lip like morning dew on a rose petal. There was an innocent expression on her face and a puzzled glint in her eyes.

He tried to reach across the table, to pull her out of danger, but before he could get a hold of her arm, a tall, powerful-looking woman stepped out of the door and leveled a weapon at him.

He froze.

The first thing Captain Proton noticed right off was that the new woman in the room wore very little clothing. In fact, that detail was hard to miss. She had on what looked to be a brass— or maybe cop- per—b o d i c e held firmly in place by leather straps over her shoulders and under her arms.  The bodice looked sharp enough to be a deadly weapon in a close, hand-to-hand fight. Captain Proton had no intention of getting close enough to find out.

Her skirt was short and golden and revealed her stomach above the waist and powerful legs below the hemline. Her hair was the color of a setting sun, almost red in its richness.

And she was tall. Taller than Captain Proton by a few inches at least.

The weapon she held was almost transparent and very, very large. Frozen in position reaching for Constance, Captain Proton found himself looking right down the very, very large barrel. He was fairly certain he could see the firing chamber inside.

Using his years of training and lightning-fast reflexes, he dove sideways just as the woman fired, exploding his chair into sawdust and spilling his bisque all over the expensive moon carpet.

As he rolled he noted that the weapon fired a high-energy pulse beam. He'd never heard or seen anything like it before. But that didn't mean much. The Galaxy was a very large place and high-energy pulse weapons were possible.

Constance screamed, stood, and tried to run.

Captain Proton rolled and came up with his ray gun, a small weapon he always kept tucked into his boot just for such emergencies, even when dressed up and dining out in a fine restaurant.

The tall woman fired at him again!

Captain Proton rolled to the left, just in time to get out of the way.

Another tall, muscular woman, dressed exactly like the first, appeared through the door and grabbed Constance by both arms, picking her up as if she weighed nothing more than a leaf. Captain Proton knew that Constance weighed a great deal more than a leaf, which made that second tall woman extremely strong.

The first tall woman fired once more!

Captain Proton rolled again and this time came up firing, making sure he didn't hit Constance. He winged the first tall woman in the arm. She spun around and smashed to the ground as two more very large, very tall women stepped through the Interspacial Door. They were all dressed the same and looked the same. And both new women had weapons drawn, aimed, and ready to fire.

Rolling out of the way wasn't going to save him this time. But he had an old saying he lived by: *When facing terrible odds and no chance of survival, doing something is better than doing nothing.*

Right now he was about to be blown into just a little more than a wet spot on the wall, a distasteful stain that would ruin a perfectly good dining room in a wonderful restaurant.

Again his instincts took over and he sprang toward the swinging door that led into the kitchen, smashing through it just as the wall behind him was destroyed by two high-energy pulse beams from the two new visitors.

Constance screamed.

Captain Proton tumbled into the kitchen and crashed into a serving table, sending dishes full of salad and shrimp flying in all directions. Two chefs started to come toward him, but he waved them back out of danger.

He shoved himself up onto one knee, picking crustaceans out of his hair, ray gun still aimed at the door, ready to take on anyone who followed him.

In the dining room, Constance screamed again. But in mid-scream the sound was cut off as if someone had stopped a recording in mid-note.

No one came through the door after him.

Then he realized what was happening. The women didn't care about him. He was expendable, something that had simply been in the way.

They wanted Constance!

Captain Proton moved quickly back to the door and pushed it open just enough to peer into the smoke-filled private dining room.

The wounded woman was being helped through the Interspacial Door by one of the similarly attired women. Two others stood guard.

There was no sign of Constance. She must have already been taken through to the other side of that portal.

Captain Proton swung the kitchen door open and fired again, hitting one attacker solidly in the brass bodice, sending her tumbling backward and through the Interspacial Cross-Galactic Door.

The remaining invader fired, exploding the door frame right above Captain Proton's head and sending him sprawling backward into the kitchen from the shock.

By the time he had scrambled to his feet and gotten back to the edge

of the now destroyed kitchen entrance, all the invaders were back through the Interspacial Cross-Galactic Door and it was shimmering, about to vanish.

They had taken Constance!

With no regard now for his personal safety, only thinking of rescuing Constance, he rushed back into the dinning room and dove full-out through the air for the shimmering Interspacial Cross-Galactic Door. His thought was to get through the Door before it closed, then deal with the women on the other side.

If he lived long enough.

Chapter 2:

OF MICE AND HUMANS

He flew over the dining-room table like a swimmer diving from the starting blocks, reaching for the blue-tinted opening where they had taken Constance.

But he wasn't fast enough.

Before he could reach the Interspacial Cross-Galactic Door with his mad dive, it shrunk to the size of a small ball, hovered in the air for just an instant, and then, with a *slurpy-pop* and a flash of blue, vanished completely.

Captain Proton landed hard, face first on the carpet, right below where the Interspacial Cross-Galactic Door had been.

Around him the silence settled over the destroyed dining room and the remains of their quiet dinner. He glanced around. No one else was in sight.

Constance had been kidnapped right out from under his gaze!

It was all his fault!

He had relaxed, let his guard down, decided to try to enjoy an evening, and that had allowed Constance to be taken.

His job was to protect the Galaxy from the Scum of the Universe. He knew it was a full-time job, twenty-four hours a day, seven days a week.

The Scum of the Universe never rested.

From now on neither would he!

He pounded his fist on the carpet, then pushed himself to his feet, a determined look covered his face like concrete hardened on a statue. He stared at the space where the Interspacial Cross-Galactic Door had been. Constance had been taken somewhere in the Galaxy. His first problem was finding out exactly where. Then he had to rescue her. But he'd worry about that when the time came.

 He put enough credits on his table to pay for both the meal and all the damage, then added a big tip before heading toward the door.

He had to act fast!

There wasn't much time!

There was no telling what those tall women in the brass bodices would do to poor Constance.

The thought made him shudder and move even faster.

In his ship at the Moon Spaceport, he told his friend, Ace Reporter Buster Kincaid what had happened to Constance.

"But how are we going to find her?" Kincaid wondered. "It's a big Galaxy out there."

"I have an idea," Captain Proton replied. "If we adjust the setting on a long range Imagizer to show only the blue spectrum of light, we might be able to trace the path of the Interspacial Cross-Galactic Door to its source."

"Easy as snapping your fingers," Kincaid replied, jumping to the panel and twisting two knobs marked IMAGIZER ADJUSTMENTS. "Done!"

Captain Proton snapped on the main Imagizer and stared at the weird vision it now showed outside. Everything was tinted blue, with no other colors showing. The big Moon Dome looked like a giant blue bubble on the blue Moon's surface.

"Wow," Kincaid emoted, "I bet you don't see the Moon like this very often."

"True," Captain Proton answered. Then he spotted what he was looking for. A faint blue line heading off into the depths of space from the area of the restaurant. The blue tint around the Interspacial Cross-Galactic Door had clued him in.

"Prepare to take off!" Proton ordered, stepping to the controls of his ship.

"Ready!" Kincaid shouted back from his panel.

"Lift off!" Proton exclaimed.

The ship rumbled, then easily left the light pull of the Moon's gravity. Proton quickly banked the ship to follow the faint blue line heading off into space. "Full power!" he ordered.

"Full Power!" Kincaid repeated, and a moment later the ship surged forward into the ether.

The blue line in space led them directly to a yellow and green planet and directly into a giant gold palace that sat up on a giant cliff.

"There's no record of this planet," Kincaid said. "I searched the entire Interplanetary Patrol's planet file."

"So we go in quiet and well-armed," Proton said, landing the ship behind some giant rocks a few miles from the huge gold palace. From space he could tell there were underground caves in those rocks that might lead up to the palace. Better than knocking on the front door he figured.

It took them only minutes to strap on Energy Ray Guns and secure the ship. Then at a fast run they made their way through the gold-glowing caves. They had brought lights, but found they

didn't need them, since something in the walls seemed to create a light all its own.

"The path is well-worn," Proton explained, pointing to the dirt ahead. "Be ready!"

Just as he said that, a blue beam of light slashed past his ear and exploded against the gold wall behind him, sending rocks spraying in all directions.

He rolled to his right while Kincaid went in the other direction. Proton came up on one knee and fired, hitting a guard solidly. Then both he and Kincaid waited, but it seemed there were no other guards down here.

A moment later they were standing over a stunned, but very beautiful giant woman wearing a brass bodice, short skirt, and gold headband. "Tie her hands and feet," Proton ordered Kincaid. "We'll free her on the way back."

Proton scouted ahead down the cave as Kincaid did as he had been told. If there was one guard, there were bound to be many more. Their odds of getting to Constance didn't seem good this way, but it was the best way he could think of.

"Captain Proton!" Kincaid's shout echoed through the cavern. "Hurry!" Then the sound of ray gun-fire and exploding rocks filled the cavern.

Proton instantly sprang back toward his friend who was fighting for his life.

Kincaid was behind a large rock, his ray gun aiming back down the cavern in the direction they had come.

"Are they coming up behind us?" Proton demanded as he ducked behind a second rock near the bound giant woman.

A half dozen *zip*like sounds filled the air and the rock in the tunnel around Proton and Kincaid splintered.

"Didn't see who was firing," Kincaid shouted over the noise.

"Nanoids," the bound giant woman said calmly. "We will be killed."

More *zip*-sounding shots cut the air around them as Captain Proton kneeled over the woman. "What are Nanoids?"

"Like you," the woman said disgustedly. "Only tiny."

"Small Earthlings?" Kincaid asked the woman, looking puzzled. "Like me?"

"Much smaller." She almost spit the words as if talking about nothing more than rats. Clearly her people and the Nanoids did not get along.

Proton returned fire down the tunnel, slowing slightly the pace of the ray gun fire that was shattering the rock and filling the tunnel with dust. But he still couldn't see what she was talking about. Humans smaller than Kincaid? What were they doing here?

"Captain!" Kincaid said. "Look!" He pointed down the tunnel.

Through the dust Proton caught a glimpse of a Nanoid. It stood no more than a foot tall at most, perfectly formed, just like the giant women, with gold skin and solid muscles. The Nanoid carried the small gun that had been making the zipping sounds when fired.

Then suddenly the floor seemed to be alive with the creatures, filling the cavern from one side to the other. And they were charging their position!

Hundreds of them!

Maybe thousands of tiny men with tiny guns!

Around them the roof of the cavern started to collapse from all the shots.

"We die now!" the giant woman declared.

Proton and Kincaid both returned the Nanoid's fire, but it didn't seem to even slow them down. The hordes of tiny gold men kept coming.

And coming.

And coming.

All of them firing. None of them stopping.

Then above Captain Proton the roof of the cavern collapsed, pouring tons of rock down on him, his trusted friend Buster Kincaid, and the giant golden woman tied at their feet.

Chapter 3:

QUEEN FOR THIS DAY

The cavern was coming down around them!

Captain Proton grabbed the giant golden woman, hefted her to his shoulder as if she were a bag of concrete, and headed away from the attacking Nanoids.

"Run!" Proton shouted for Buster Kincaid to follow him through the cave toward the castle.

Behind them the tiny men called Nanoids kept firing and firing.

Zip!

Zip!

Zip! Rocks exploded.

The ground rumbled. Those tiny weapons certainly had a lot of power.

The running was hard with the giant woman over his shoulder, but Captain Proton couldn't leave her there to be killed by falling rock or hordes of tiny golden men. He had never left a woman behind and no matter what the size or strength of the woman he carried now, he wasn't about to start.

Behind them a mighty crash shook the ground as the cave collapsed.

He stumbled, but managed to not fall under his heavy burden, then kept running.

The *zip-zip-zip* of the Nanoid's guns stopped.

Proton managed to stagger another hundred running steps before dumping the bound huge woman on her seat against the cave wall.

"We make our stand here!" he ordered.

Kincaid took up a position behind a boulder on one side of the rock tunnel and Proton did the same on the other, guarding where they had just come.

Nothing moved except a distant cloud of dust.

"Seems like the cave-in stopped them," Proton observed.

"That it does," Kincaid said.

Proton stood, put his gun away and turned around to face ten very large golden women, all wearing brass bodices and short skirts, all pointing weapons at him.

Very large weapons. The same kind the women had pointed at him in the restaurant on the Moon.

"It seems," he commented, "that we have found those we were looking for."

"Or they found us," Kincaid whispered back.

"Don't kill them," the tied-up woman ordered the other women. "They saved me from the Nanoid attack. Queen Fems must know of this!"

The woman on the ground was untied and Captain Proton and Buster Kincaid were led quickly through the rest of the cave and up into the castle.

There, in a massive gold room,

covered in thick carpet and fancy drapes, was Queen Fems. She was sitting on a massive gold throne,  a golden headdress towering above her head.

Beside her stood Constance G o o d h e a r t, looking small and very scared, yet still strikingly beautiful.

Proton and Kincaid were led forward and forced to stand before the Queen.

"Have they hurt you?" Proton asked Constance.

Before she had a chance to answer the Queen held up her hand. "We had no intention of hurting her before you got here, Captain Proton."

"You know who I am?" Proton asked, astounded.

"Of course I do," the Queen replied. "You are the most famous of all the *men* in the Galaxy."

Proton noticed that she almost spit out the word *men*.

"So why did you take Constance Goodheart?" Proton demanded. He'd have put his hands on his hips in a show of defiance, but they were tied behind him. So instead he jutted his chin forward.

"To bring you here, of course," the Queen laughed. "Bait for my trap, as they say."

"Why me?" Proton demanded.

"Killing you will warn the rest of the Galaxy to not take me lightly," the Queen answered. "I will rule and even men will follow me."

"Just as the Nanoids do now," Proton retorted.

He had clearly hit a sore spot. The Queen's golden complexion grew red. Then she stood, somehow managing to not tip forward under the huge headdress.

"Silence, scum," she shouted. "Remove them from my sight. Prepare them for the Trundle Spider!"

Constance Goodheart screamed!

The Queen waved her silent. "Don't worry my dear. You're going with them."

Constance screamed again.

The guards shoved Proton, Kincaid, and Constance down a long hall, then down a flight of stairs into a room with stakes around the outside. Proton noticed instantly that the walls were splattered with blood and the floor was littered with bones. A lot of beings had died in this room, some recently. This Queen was a very blood-thirsty ruler, of that there was no doubt.

Constance looked around at all the blood and bones and screamed again, the sound echoing upward, drawing Proton's gaze that way. The room was an open pit with no real ceiling. The Queen and hundreds of other giant women in brass bodices and short skirts were gathering around the edge, getting ready to watch whatever was about to happen.

"I think we're doomed!" Kincaid exclaimed.

Constance screamed again, struggling as the giant women tied her to a stake, her arms behind her back, the rope around the stake.

Then they tied Kincaid.

Then they tied Captain Proton.

Then they quickly left the room, closing a massive stone door behind them.

"The Galaxy will know of my power now!" the Queen exclaimed from above.

Proton glanced up. "Excuse me," he said in a calm voice that carried to all the onlookers above. "You might want to stand back from the edge up there."

"Why is that?" the Queen demanded.

"I can see up your skirt," Proton answered, averting his eyes as any gentleman would do.

Kincaid did the same thing.

Constance screamed again.

As one, all the giant women above them took a step back from the edge, their hands going to their skirts as one, as if the move had been practiced in military school.

Proton winked at Kincaid. He really couldn't see up their skirts, but small victories were better than no victory, he always said.

But, it looked as if it might be his last victory.

"Release the Trundle Spider!" the Queen ordered, her face now even redder than before.

A rumbling shook the ground in front of them as a large chunk of rock moved aside, showing a black opening beyond. The odor of rotting meat filled the area.

"Yuck!" Kincaid exclaimed.

"Someone needs to throw out the trash," Proton commented.

Above them a hush fell over the crowd of giant golden women as a rustling noise came from the newly opened door.

"I think we're about to have a visitor," Proton noted.

Suddenly a large bulk filled the door as a massive, hairy spider appeared. This thing was bigger than a house and smelled worse than a city dump. A dozen red eyes seemed to spin around and around in the center of its ugly face.

Constance screamed.

Kincaid struggled at his ropes.

Proton fought to escape, to get away from the post, but he was tied firmly.

The spider moved out in front of them, its smell overwhelming them, its rotating twelve eyes getting closer, like a nightmare that wouldn't go away. In all his years of space travel, Captain Proton had never seen anything so hideously ugly.

Constance screamed again.

"Say hello to your executioner, Captain Proton!" the Queen exclaimed, then laughed wildly.

The Trundle Spider towered over them. Saliva dripped from its huge mouth. A simple flick from one of its many legs would kill them instantly.

"Kill them!" the Queen ordered from above.

The Trundle Spider glanced up at the Queen, then stepped closer to Captain Proton.

"We're doomed!" Kincaid shouted, still fighting to get out of his bonds without luck.

Constance screamed.

The giant spider moved closer.

And closer.

And closer.

Chapter 4:
A MAN'S BEST FRIEND

The giant Trundle Spider stalked Captain Proton and his friends like a cat savoring the capture of a mouse. The smell of rot choked Captain Proton's nose and mouth as he worked frantically at his bonds, but they didn't feel as if they were coming loose anytime in the near future.

Above them Queen Fems and her loyal subjects were cheering, as if what was going on below were a close game and their home team was leading. Captain Proton could see nothing sporting about this at all.

The Giant Trundle Spider got closer and closer, then finally leaned down so that its revolving red eyes were only a foot in front of Captain Proton's face. For some reason, it seemed to be studying

him before it killed him. The smell made Proton's stomach turn. Luckily he hadn't eaten much for breakfast.

Then a tiny voice whispered from the Giant Trundle Spider's mouth, "Are you really Captain Proton, that hero guy that everyone's always talkin' about?"

Proton stared into the twirling eyes, for the first time seeing a real brain behind their whirling redness.

"I am Captain Proton of the Patrol," he replied, keeping his head bowed to make sure no one above could see him talking. "Who are you?"

"I am called by many names," the Giant Trundle Spider whispered. "My mother called me Phred. It kinda suits me, don't ya think?"

"It does at that," Proton answered.

"Thanks." Phred the Giant Trundle Spider sounded pleased that Captain Proton had liked his name.

Proton glanced at Kincaid who was looking completely stunned, just like Proton was feeling at the moment.

He turned back to the awful smell of the giant spider and looked it square in its swirling eyes. "Phred, you know you're supposed to eat us?" Proton reminded the Giant Spider. "Is there anything I can do to change that?"

"Hold on to your shirt there,"

Phred the Giant Spider whispered. "Got to put on a show for the crowd. Show business, don't you know. No rest for the weary."

He reared back and stalked around the room, his many legs thrashing, his feet kicking up dirt. But Captain Proton noted that as the women above them cheered his movements, Phred was very careful to not touch him or Kincaid or Constance.

Then, just for good measure, Phred went real close to Constance and she screamed.

The women above actually applauded.

Then Phred put his twirling red eyes right down in front of Proton again. "I might be able to help you if you help me escape this prison. You know it's just awful here. The place stinks all the time. The food is bad. I get no respect. You just don't know."

"I think I can help," Proton reassured, glancing at Kincaid who was still looking stunned.

"Then we got us a deal?" Phred asked.

"We do," Proton answered.

"Okay, look," Phred responded. "I brought a couple weapons, little things I snatched from guards but can't use. I figure the screamer doesn't need one."

"But she must come with us," Proton demanded.

"Sure, sure," Phred answered, kicking up dirt with four of his hind legs for those above to see.

"No skin off my thorax. I'll cut you all loose, drop the weapons at your feet and then head for my den. You follow. Got it? That Queen won't dare follow right off."

"Buy us some time?" Proton asked.

"Exactly," the Giant Spider whispered. "Now all of you hold still."

"Do as he says," Proton ordered Kincaid and Constance.

Both nodded.

"Show time!" Phred snorted.

With a sudden flurry of movement the Giant Trundle Spider started to move, around and around the three prisoners, back and forth, its legs moving so fast that Captain Proton couldn't follow them. Then suddenly Proton's hands were free as one of Phred's legs cut the ropes perfectly.

Dust filled the air.

Phred kept moving.

Above them the giant women cheered what they thought were the deaths of Captain Proton and his friends.

A weapon dropped in the dirt at Proton's feet, then another in front of Kincaid.

Proton grabbed the weapon, then shouted to Kincaid as the Giant Spider headed for the opening to its den in the side of the rock, kicking up as much dust as it could on the way.

"Follow Phred!" Proton ordered.

Kincaid grabbed the weapon at his feet and did as he had been told.

At a run Proton scooped up the light figure of Constance Goodheart and ran behind Kincaid. For a moment the dust covered their escape, but then a stunned silence fell over the crowd above as they saw what was happening.

"Stop them!" The Queen's demanding order echoed over the pit.

Proton barely reached the safety of the Giant Spider's den as the pit exploded in shots fired from above. Then slowly the rock door closed, sealing them in the Spider's den and cutting off the sound of the shots and the Queen's angry orders.

Proton put Constance down and turned to face the twirling eyes of the Giant Spider.

"My, now that was exciting, wasn't it?" Phred exclaimed, his two front legs rubbing together. "I think we made the Queen just a touch angry, now don't you?"

"Do you have a way out of here?" Proton asked calmly, fearing the answer the Spider was going to give.

"If I did, would I still be hanging around here?" Phred snorted, his eyes twirling even faster. "That's why I needed your help."

"Okay," Proton agreed. "Is there another way besides the pit back there?"

"Sure," the Giant Spider answered. He turned and glided across the bone-strewn cave until he reached a seemingly solid rock wall. "That opens." He touched it with one of his many legs. "That's how they got me in here."

"Where does it lead?" Proton asked.

"Through a big cave to a beautiful meadow below the Castle," Phred replied almost wistfully, if a Giant Spider could be wistful. Proton was sure that if any Spider could be, it was Phred.

Proton checked the weapon in his hand. As he suspected, it was just like the ones the golden women had fired at him in the restaurant. High-energy pulse beams. Very powerful.

"Phred, stand back with Constance," Proton ordered.

Phred moved back and Constance moved to one side, staying away from the giant, red-eyed Spider.

Proton scratched a large mark on the rock, then stepped back. With a click he adjusted the weapon to full-energy blast. "Kincaid, put your weapon on full and on my mark fire at that spot."

"Understood," Kincaid answered. "But you know we might bring this cave right down on top of us."

"I know," Proton stated. "But it's better than the alternative, don't you think? You agree, Phred?"

"Of course, of course. Hurry up, would ya? We don't got all day."

"You heard the Giant Spider," Proton ordered. "Fire!"

Instantly the rock exploded where the two weapons beams struck. Dust filled the chamber, causing Kincaid to cough. The roof didn't come down, but they also didn't break out either. But there was a large hole in the stone.

"Do it again!" Proton commanded. "This time keep firing until we see daylight!"

"Ready!" Kincaid shouted.

"Fire!"

Energy pulse after energy pulse pounded into the rock, sending dust everywhere.

Around them the ground shook.

The noise was so loud Proton wondered if he would ever hear well again.

Constance screamed, but it sounded far off in the distance because of all the pounding of the pulse beams into the rock.

"Not looking good!" Phred shouted.

"Keep firing!" Proton ordered Kincaid, holding the trigger on his blaster down, hoping the charge in the weapon would last long enough.

The ground shook even more.

Dust filled the air.

Rocks from the ceiling started to fall.

Then, as the entire den started to collapse on them, Constance screamed again.

To come so far to die here didn't seem right to Captain Proton. But as the rocks rained on him from above, it didn't seem as if he was going to have much choice in the matter.

Not much choice at all.

Chapter 5:

A COMET A DAY

It's open!" Phred, the Giant Trundle Spider shouted as the roof of his prison fell on them, one rock at a time. Through the dust Proton could see the Giant Spider scrambling over the fallen rocks and through a large hole in the wall that they had made with the energy weapons.

Captain Proton managed to shove Constance through the hole, then followed behind Kincaid, tumbling out on the other side on the floor of a large, rock-strewn cave.

Shots bounced off the rocks as Queen Fems' guards fired on them.

Both Kincaid and Captain Proton dove for cover and returned fire as Phred ran down the corridor toward the distant daylight like a child let out of school on the first day of summer.

"Cover him!" Proton ordered.

"Thanks, Captain Proton!" Phred shouted as he ran, all his legs a blur of speed and power. Almost instantly the Giant Trundle Spider squeezed through the end of the cave and disappeared.

"Follow him, Constance!" Proton ordered. "We'll cover you!"

Constance took off running, staying low as Captain Proton and Buster Kincaid fired at Queen Fems' guard's position up the cave, not giving them time to fire back.

Proton watched until he was sure Constance was clear, then shouted to Kincaid, "Run for it!"

Kincaid turned and headed down the corridor as Proton covered him, exploding rocks in front of Queen's guards, knocking two of the bodice wearing women over backward.

Then Kincaid took up a position behind a huge boulder and covered Proton as he retreated.

Shortly, leapfrogging their way down through the cave, they made it to the rock face overlooking the beautiful valley and the massive forest below. The fresh air and sunlight was like a wake-up call to Captain Proton. Twice in the last hour he had thought he might never see daylight again. He just wished he had time to enjoy it right now, but with the Queen angry and her guards right  behind them, there wasn't much time at all.

Below them in the valley was a giant forest. They had come out on the wrong side of the mountain from their ship. Somehow they had to go all the way around to get

there. Going back through the Queen's castle certainly wasn't an option.

There was no sign of Phred, the Giant Trundle Spider. Captain Proton doubted they would ever see their friend again. No doubt he was miles away from this mountain already and gaining speed. And Captain Proton didn't blame him at all. He hadn't eaten them. They had released him. A fair trade by any standards.

"We have to get off this mountain and fast," Proton observed as shots cut into the rocks from the cave mouth behind them. "Into the forest for cover."

They managed to keep behind large rocks all the way to the edge of the forest.

It was a green place, after all the browns and golds of the Queen's palace on the mountain above. Giant trees thrust into the air twenty stories tall, with trunks as big around as a city block on the bottom. They certainly didn't make anything small, except the Nanoids, on this planet.

Around the huge trees the forest floor was mostly bare, except for some large fernlike plants. The deeper they went into the forest, the darker it got as the huge trees blocked more and more of the sunlight.

"I don't think we should go much farther in," Kincaid worried aloud.

"Agreed," Proton said. "Turn

right and we'll follow the edge of the forest along the base of the mountain until we come near our ship."

"Great idea!" Kincaid retorted. "The ridges in the bark of these monster trees is rough enough and deep enough for us to hide in if we need to."

Captain Proton had already noted that, but didn't tell his friend so.

"Okay, let's get moving," Proton said, shoving Kincaid along. "We don't want to be in this forest when the sun goes down. From the size of Phred and these trees, there's no telling how large the animals can get on this planet."

"Hadn't thought of that," Kincaid whispered, looking around, his gun at the ready.

Constance looked as if she was going to scream.

"Don't worry," Proton reassured his friends. "We can be at the ship before dark if we get moving now."

"Then what are we waiting for?" Kincaid asked, turning and walking off on a course that led along the base of the Queen's mountain.

Proton motioned that Constance should follow Kincaid, then he brought up the rear, keeping a sharp lookout for the Queen's guards or any large creature.

They made good time and just as the sun was setting, they reached their ship. The last climb up the rocks and over the ridge where the Nanoids had attacked them was done slowly and silently. Along the way they had avoided three of the Queen's guards and seen no giant beasts, although Captain Proton was sure that a number of times they were being watched by something in the trees above.

"Feels great to be back!" Kincaid exclaimed as they entered the ship.

"Stand by for take-off!" Proton ordered.

"Standing by!" Kincaid replied.

"Blast off!" Proton shouted over the roar of the jets as their ship thrust them away from the planet and into space.

Suddenly the Imagizer came on in front of Captain Proton. The face of Queen Fems filled the space. "I see you have escaped my prison. But you know you won't get far. I will soon control all of the Galaxy."

"I've heard that before," Proton replied calmly, acting almost bored. "From far more powerful beings than you, my dear Queen Fems."

Again her face grew red, almost matching the color of her bright red hair. She seemed to sputter, then said smartly, "We shall see about that!"

She cut off her image.

"She's not so good with a retort," Kincaid laughed.

"But we need to stay alert!" Proton reminded his friend. "Her bite may be worse than her rhetoric."

"You're right!" Kincaid shouted,

staring at the Imagizer. "We have company all around us!"

Captain Proton stared at the screen, not really believing what he was seeing: Comets. Hundreds of comets coming at them from all directions, their tails fanning out great distances behind them.

"Not possible!" Captain Proton stated matter-of-factly. "Comets remain in set orbits and need the sun's energy to create their tails. They are not alive and do not fly under their own power at all."

"These comets look alive!" Kincaid shouted.

Just then their ship shook as one of the comets fired at them. Sparks flew from the panels and smoke poured out of the controls where Kincaid stood.

"Comets with weapons!" Proton shouted. "What next?"

Constance screamed.

Suddenly on the Imagizer the face of Queen Fems appeared again. "Now who's laughing, Captain Proton? See if you can escape my Comet Killers as easily as you escaped my prison!"

She laughed a truly evil laugh, then her face vanished as another blast from the Comet Killers rocked their ship, sending them all tumbling to the deck.

Captain Proton and Kincaid were first back to their feet and their stations.

"We're completely surrounded!" Kincaid shouted.

Proton could see that. At least fifty comets were closing in on them, impossible as that seemed. Over the years he had fought many different kinds of ships, but never a comet. What kind of power did they use? What kind of weapons did they have? Too many questions.

"Return fire!" he ordered, swerving the ship to the right and giving it full power.

"Firing!" Kincaid shouted as two more blasts rocked their ship.

Again Constance screamed.

"Direct hit!" Kincaid shouted.

But Captain Proton could clearly see it made no difference. The comet they had hit simply kept coming onward. They were surrounded by comets on all sides.

More blasts rocked the ship.

Then more, sending the entire ship into darkness.

Constance screamed!

Then one more mighty blast sent them tumbling uncontrollably through space right at a nearby moon. Captain Proton knew they would never survive the impact.

Furiously Captain Proton fought to regain power and control of his ship as the moon loomed larger.

And larger.

And larger.

The moon's craters smiled at them as if welcoming them to their deaths.

Chapter 6:

THE MOON IS A NASTY QUEEN

The Queen's Comet Killers swarmed around Captain Proton's ship like birds with long tails around a feeder. Shot after shot after shot rocked Proton's ship, pounding away at his thick hull.

Smoke filled the room, yet Captain Proton and Buster Kincaid fought on, never giving up as Constance Goodheart hung on for dear life near the hatch.

"Our ship can't take much more of this pounding!" Kincaid shouted as another blast shook them like an angry man might shake a salt shaker.

"I know!" Proton answered, yanking the control hard left. "I'm going to make a run for that nearby moon. It has an atmosphere. Maybe they can't follow us down there!"

"Great thinking!" Kincaid exclaimed.

"Full speed!" Proton ordered.

Kincaid twisted the dial, giving the ship all the power he could.

More blasts from the Comet Killers smashed into them, but Proton managed to keep the ship under control, fighting the levers like the master pilot that he was.

Suddenly there was a large bump and their hull started to heat up, turning red.

"We've entered the moon's atmosphere!" Kincaid shouted. "The Comet Killers are not following!"

"Hold on!" Proton ordered. "We came in too fast! This is going to be a rough landing!"

He was right.

It was a very rough landing.

The ship bounced twice through the trees before coming to rest against a large rock. Kincaid and Constance were both tossed to the deck, but Captain Proton was quickly relieved to find out both were all right.

With a few pops and hisses from the craft, Proton shut off the ship. The silence seemed almost louder than the explosions, the atmosphere pounding on the hull, and the crash landing all combined.

"Were we followed down?" Proton asked, turning from his pilot's controls.

Kincaid scrambled back to the Space Tracking and Viewing board and studied it for a moment, then smiled at Proton. "No! The Comet Killers have formed a large cloud and are heading off into space."

"Toward where?" Proton demanded.

Kincaid studied the Space Tracking control for a moment longer, then again looked up at Captain Proton. But this time he was no longer smiling.

"The Comet Killers are heading for Epsey Second Prime."

"The Patrol has a huge base there!" Proton exclaimed, very

worried. "If that base is taken the Incorporated Planets might fall to the forces of evil!"

"But how can we stop the Comet Killers?" Kincaid wondered aloud, looking around at the mess. "Our ship is too damaged to fly!"

"Then we'll fix it!" Proton stated firmly. "Kincaid, work on the engine. I'll work on the weapons. Constance, you scout around the ship checking for hull damage. Everyone understand their duty?"

Both Kincaid and Constance nodded.

"Well snap to it!" Proton ordered. "The Patrol needs us in the fight against the Comet Killers."

Quickly they all went to work.

Soon Captain Proton had the weapons repaired and recharged to full power.

A moment later Kincaid crawled out from under the engine and wiped some grease off his hands. "Engine's ready!"

Suddenly from outside the ship Constance screamed.

Both men sprang into movement toward the door, with Captain Proton going outside first, his weapon drawn and ready to fire.

She was nowhere to be seen.

"Constance!" Captain Proton shouted, his voice echoing off the forest and rocks around the ship.

Constance screamed again, this time from a little farther away through the trees. "Guard the ship!" Proton ordered Kincaid. "This might be a trap!"

"Understood!" Kincaid answered, moving back and taking up a defensive position just inside the hatch.

Captain Proton, with a mighty bound, jumped over some nearby brush and hit the ground running in the direction of Constance's last scream.

But he was too late.

Just as he entered the trees, the ground shook and in a clearing ahead he could see the orange and red flames of a rocket ship taking off. He knew at once that Constance was on board.

She had been kidnapped again.

Without a moment's hesitation he turned around and was quickly back inside his ship, with Kincaid closing the door. They were going after whoever had taken Constance.

Then, just before they were about to take off, the face of Queen Fems again filled his Imagizer. She was laughing.

"Captain Proton," the Queen cackled. "I see I again have something you want."

The Queen flicked a switch and the image of Constance Goodheart, tied to a chair, came into focus. Clearly she was on the ship that had just taken off.

"Get ready for launch!" Proton ordered Kincaid.

The Queen's image came back. "That won't be necessary," she warned. "I want you to watch my Magic Glass Jewel at work and see why."

The Queen touched a glass orb on a bracelet on her arm.

The Image switched back to Constance. Behind her, just as in the restaurant, an Insterspacial Cross-Galactic Door formed and two large women stepped out. They picked up Constance, chair and all, and stepped back through the door.

Then the Queen's face appeared on the Imagizer again. Constance sat beside the Queen in the palace, bound and gagged. The Queen held up her Magic Glass Jewel on the bracelet. "Thought you might find that interesting," she said smoothly.

Then slowly she broke into a cackling laughter and, a moment later, cut the connection.

Both Captain Proton and Buster Kincaid stood stunned.

Then Kincaid observed. "Now we know how she controls the Interspacial Cross-Galactic Doors."

"There's something very strange going on here," Proton observed.

"How's that?" Kincaid asked.

"I'm not exactly sure," Proton replied, deep in thought. "But there seems to be something bigger happening than just a mad Queen trying for Galaxy-wide domination. And I intend to find out what!"

"So back to the Queen's palace!" Kincaid exclaimed.

"No," Proton stated flatly. "That is exactly what she wants us to do. But we have a bigger job!"

"Bigger than saving Constance?" Kincaid asked, clearly stunned.

"Yes," Proton responded flatly, keeping all emotion from his voice. "For the moment she is safe. The Queen must have her as bait to lure us. Constance won't be harmed until we are there."

"But we won't be lured," Kincaid defied.

"Exactly!" Proton exclaimed. "She wants us to come there, but our duty is to help the Patrol against the Comet Killers. Prepare for launch!"

Kincaid jumped to his position as Captain Proton stood at his controls, his powerful hands grasping the levers. The Imagizer in front of him showed only empty space. It took great courage to leave Constance Goodheart in the clutches of the evil Queen Fems.

But he must.

He must.

"Launch!" he ordered.

Under them the rockets rumbled as the ship lifted into space.

In front of them lay a great duty to all of the Galaxy and the Patrol. And as the famous saying went, "Sometimes the good of the many outweighs the good of the one."

Captain Proton lived by those words. He knew that after all the years of being his secretary, Constance Goodheart understood them too.

Chapter 7:

A LITTLE HELP

"Comet Killers are approaching the Patrol base!" Kincaid exclaimed.

On the Imagizer in front of Captain Proton he could see the massive Comet Killers, their long tails swaying off behind them like feathers on a peacock. There were hundreds of them and they had surrounded the entire Patrol Fleet and were about ready to attack. Captain Proton had seen worse odds before, but this looked really bad for the Patrol.

As he watched, the Comet Killers spread out, taking up what looked to be a standard attack formation. They looked like comets, but acted like warships.

"How long until we get there?" Proton demanded.

"Almost there!" Kincaid answered.

Suddenly everything seemed to freeze.

The Comet Killers.

The Patrol ships.

Even Proton's ship.

Everything around them just stopped.

No rumble of the engine.

No whine of the Space Drive.

Nothing moved.

"What happened?" Kincaid whispered, fear clearly filling his voice in the sudden silence around them.

"I don't know!" Proton respond-

ed firmly, looking around, then back up at the Imagizer. "It seems time has stopped for some reason."

Then, out of the corner of his eye, Captain Proton caught a glimpse of something forming near the post where Constance usually stood.

He drew his gun and spun just as a man wearing a black suit stepped through what looked like a circular, green, Cross-Galactic Door. The man had a stern face, snow white hair, and bright green eyes when he took off his sunglasses. He smiled at Captain Proton, ignoring the gun.

"What are you doing on my ship?" Captain Proton demanded sternly.

The man again smiled, sort of a fond smile of a grandfather staring at a grandchild. "I've come to help, of course. And from the looks of the coming battle, I'd say you are going to need it."

"Who are you?" Kincaid asked. "Did you freeze time?"

The man laughed a soft laugh that Captain Proton found somewhat reassuring for a reason he didn't understand.

"Time isn't stopped," the man answered. "No being in all of creation has the ability to do that. I simply pulled you and Captain Proton between moments so we could have the luxury of speaking before the fighting."

"Oh," Kincaid said, clearly not understanding.

Seemed like freezing time to

Captain Proton, but he said nothing about that point. "You didn't answer my friend's first question," Proton reminded the silver-haired man in the black suit. "Exactly who are you?"

"My name is not understandable in your language. You can simply call me Folke if you must attach a name."

"*People's Guardian* in Scandinavian," Captain Proton explained.

The old man smiled and nodded, as if proud of the fact that Captain Proton had caught him. "You see many things, Captain Proton. It is why I came to talk to you."

"I am listening," Proton said without emotion. Around them time seemed to remain frozen. Or as the guy explained, they stayed outside of it.

"I think," Folke said, "that first we must deal with the problem at hand." He gestured toward the Imagizer and the frozen Comet Killers about ready to destroy an important Patrol base and fleet.

"Please," Proton agreed.

"Those Comet Killers, as they are called by the person who sent them against you, are not live creatures or freaks of nature. They are nothing more than elaborate spaceships, disguised to appear as comets."

"I assumed as much," Proton assured Folke.

"But you did not know that the ship itself is not in the head of the comet, but directly behind the head

in the thickest part of the tail. The head is just an illusion."

"Good information."

"That's why our shots didn't hurt them," Kincaid exclaimed.

"Exactly my young friend," Folke chortled. "The ships inside the comets are powerful, but so are your Patrol ships. The fight should be a fair one."

"Now that we know where they are," Proton agreed.

"We will talk again." Folke bowed slightly, turned and stepped through a green circular door that had opened almost instantly directly behind him.

"Wait!" Proton shouted, but he was too late.

The man was gone.

The door was gone.

No noise, no green light, nothing.

Suddenly the ship seemed to lurch as time started to move again around them. Or, as Folke said, they again joined up with the time stream. It seemed the same either way.

"The engine is running perfectly," Kincaid reported after a quick check.

"Tell all the other Patrol ships what Folke told us!" Captain Proton ordered. "Be prepared to fire on my command!"

It took Kincaid only a moment to

relay the message to all the other Patrol ships. Then he shouted, "Ready!"

Captain Proton dove his ship right at the nearest Comet Killer. "Target the tail behind the comet's head and fire!"

"Firing!" Kincaid said as their power beam shot out and smashed into the comet's tail. The comet seemed to suddenly turn.

It flickered, like a light bulb about ready to burn out.

Then the comet vanished, leaving only a gray, thin ship in its stead.

"Direct hit!" Kincaid celebrated.

"Keep firing!" Proton ordered.

Shortly the remaining Comet Killers were retreating, with Patrol ships hot on their tails.

The Patrol base was safe!

It was now time to go get Constance!

He quickly banked the ship and set course for Queen Fems' planet. "Full speed ahead!" Proton ordered.

Suddenly, right in front of them a giant Blue Whirlpool formed, spinning like the dreaded Space Vortex of Doom. But that couldn't be the Space Vortex of Doom. It was on the other side of Earth, far away from this location.

And it wasn't blue.

"Watch out!" Kincaid shouted a warning.

Captain Proton shoved the control levers hard right, trying to spin the ship enough to miss the swirling Blue Whirlpool that had appeared in front of them. It looked familiar, as if he'd seen it before.

"We're going in!" Kincaid shouted the obvious.

Proton fought to keep their ship out!

There had to be something he could do!

Anything?

He flipped the ship over and headed them directly away from the swirling blue mass. Then he shouted, "Full power!"

The ship surged against the pull of the swirling Blue Whirlpool as Kincaid turned the dial that gave the ship full power.

For an instant Captain Proton thought they may have enough power to pull free as the ship inched forward.

Slower.

Slower.

Then the ship stopped.

The maneuver hadn't worked!

"Any more power?"

"None!" Kincaid yelled back as the ship started to shake and rumble with the intense forces pulling and shoving at it.

The swirling Blue Whirlpool pulled at it.

The engines shoved the ship in the other direction. It was lucky to be holding together!

Slowly, very slowly, the ship was pulled backward, against the full power of the drive.

The swirling Blue Whirlpool was too much for them!

They were being sucked down inside, surrounded by blue as if they were swimming in water too deep to see the bottom.

The ship shook.

Rattled!

Panels fell from the ceiling!

It was about ready to tear itself apart.

They only had a few seconds to live!

Something had to be done!

"The pressure on the outside of the hull is starting to build!" Kincaid pushed. "It's going to smash us!"

Knowing they only had a few seconds left, Captain Proton made the only choice he could. He spun the ship around and at full power headed straight down into the blue, swirling mass.

"What are you doing?" Kincaid asked, his shout barely audible over the rumbling of the ship. "We'll be crushed by the intense gravity!"

Captain Proton kept his steely gaze locked firmly on the Imagizer and the swirling blue point ahead.

"Let's hope not!" he shouted back.

If they were going to be killed, they would die taking action, not running away from the danger.

"Five seconds until the hull collapses!" Kincaid shouted another warning.

Captain Proton ignored his friend's call, aiming his ship for the very center of the Blue Whirlpool.

With the engines on full and the attraction force of the Blue Whirlpool, they were traveling faster than any ship had ever gone before.

On the Imagizer the swirls of the Blue Whirlpool blurred as they went down, faster.

Faster.

Faster.

Down into the unknown.

Down into the heart of blueness.

Chapter 8:

WHERE NO CAPTAIN HAS GONE BEFORE

With the ship rumbling and shaking around him, Captain Proton aimed the nose of the ship directly at the center of the swirling Blue Whirlpool of madness that surrounded them.

"Hold on!" he shouted to his friend, Buster Kincaid.

The next instant they flashed through the center of the Blue Whirlpool and were back in normal space.

The normal stars looked wonderful!

They had survived!

"Cut power!" Proton ordered, staring at the Imagizer in front of him. The swirling Blue Whirlpool was now gone, vanished as fast as it had appeared.

"Power cut!" Kincaid answered.

Around them the ship went silent as Kincaid moved up beside Captain Proton to stare at the Imagizer.

Proton couldn't believe what he was seeing. At first glance everything looked normal. Stars, blackness of space, a planet or two circling nearby suns. But these weren't the stars or the world of the Incorporated Planets.

These weren't even the stars of his Galaxy!

Somehow the Blue Whirlpool had transported them a long ways from home.

Or maybe even into another universe.

He didn't know how or why, for that matter. But Captain Proton trusted his eyes and right now they were telling him he was in an area of space he'd never seen before.

"Where are we?" Kincaid whispered, clearly seeing the same thing.

"I don't know," Proton answered. "Dig out the space maps and let's see what we can find."

"Good idea!" Kincaid emoted, then scrambled to get the maps out from under one panel. He quickly spread them out on the tool table, carefully unrolling each as if their lives might depend on it. They actually might.

Captain Proton joined him and slowly, carefully, they went through each map, looking for any planet, any star cluster, any nebula that might look similar to what they were seeing on the Imagizer.

Nothing.

They were outside of all mapped space!

The Blue Whirlpool had somehow taken them a very long ways from home. Rescuing Constance Goodheart from the clutches of the evil Queen Fems was going to be even harder now.

So on to plan number two!

"Kincaid," Captain Proton ordered, "make the same adjustments to the Imagizer that you made when we traced the Cross-Galactic Door to rescue Constance."

"You think we may have been transported by a giant Cross-Galactic Door?" Kincaid wondered, jumping to his panel to do the adjustments.

"We might have been," Proton answered.

"Adjustments finished," Kincaid announced.

They both looked at the Imagizer. As Proton had hoped, a faint blue line headed off into deep space from their present location. It *had* been a giant door that had taken them.

But why? Captain Proton wondered to himself, staring at the blue line.

And who had the power to do such a thing?

And an even bigger question, why did they want him so far out of the way? They had better hurry and get back before it was too late.

"I'll make note of the heading," Captain Proton announced. "You adjust the Imagizer to long distance magnification. I want to try to see how far we are from home."

Almost instantly Kincaid announced, "Adjustments finished!"

Captain Proton twisted the dials, working to get an image of the distant space of the Incorporated Planets. Finally, after much adjusting, he got a reading.

"Oh, no!" Kincaid exclaimed, standing beside him.

Captain Proton felt crushed, as if a weight had dropped on his chest. He forced himself to take a deep breath and look at the distance he had figured.

He was right!

Numbers didn't lie!

He did the figures again.

Same result!

Home was impossibly far away. It was no wonder none of these stars or planets were on their maps. No man had ever been here before that he knew of.

"At top speed," Kincaid wailed, "it's going to take us years to get home!"

"Seventy years to be exact," Captain Proton advised calmly.

"Seventy years?" Kincaid whispered his question. "Can that be true?"

"If we're going to rescue Con-

stance," Proton stated, taking a deep breath and facing the problem head on, "we're going to have to speed that up some, don't you think?"

Kincaid only nodded, clearly still stunned.

"And think about this," Proton demanded of Kincaid, "if someone else has the power to send us this far, we have the power to get back."

"In time to rescue Constance?" Kincaid wondered aloud.

"In time to rescue Constance," Proton assured.

"Do you have any ideas how we're going to get back?"

"A couple," Proton stated flatly, turning back to the Imagizer. He quickly brought the focus back to the space surrounding them. "But first I want to know why here?"

"What?" Kincaid asked, clearly puzzled.

"Why not send us even farther?" Proton asked, searching space around them with the Imagizer.

"Maybe they didn't have enough of that blue power?" Kincaid theorized.

"Did it look as if they were short of power?" Proton laughed.

"No," Kincaid admitted. "Maybe this far is the maximum distance the Blue Whirlpool could send a ship our size?"

"Maybe," Proton admitted. "That might be the reason. But I would wager there is another reason we were sent here. I believe we're pawns in some much bigger game and this is just a move in that game?"

"Bigger game?" Kincaid puzzled. "What bigger game?"

"There!" Proton exclaimed, pointing at the Imagizer. A giant round Space Net was bearing down on them, pulled by eighteen small ships that looked more like balls than spaceships.

"Are they the bigger game?" Kincaid demanded.

"I doubt it," Proton answered, quickly working the Imagizer to focus more clearly on the coming Space Net. "I would suspect they are just other pawns like us."

"I'm confused," Kincaid muttered.

"I will explain later!" Proton stated flatly, finally getting the image he wanted.

A Space Net is usually small and pulled by two or three ships to collect space garbage. But this one was a huge, perfectly round net that looked more like a giant golf ball floating in space. And it was clearly intented to collect them.

"Man your station!" Proton shouted.

Kincaid jumped to his position as Proton took the controls.

"We're going to have to outrun it!" Proton observed. "Full speed!"

The engines roared to life and the ship darted off, away from the Space Net.

"Their gaining!" Kincaid warned.

"More power!" Proton ordered

Kincaid turned up the engine power as far as it would go. But it soon became clear to Captain Proton that the ships pulling the Space Net were much, much faster than his ship.

He banked hard to the right, trying to see if he could outmaneuver the Space Net and the eighteen ships pulling it.

They were also quicker!

Turning as one unit, they never let the net show any slack at all. Impressive flying, he had to admit.

"Prepare the energy weapons!" Proton ordered.

"Armed and ready!" Kincaid reported back.

"Hold on!" he shouted. Then he shoved his control lever over completely, sending the ship tumbling through space for a moment until he righted it, headed right back at the center of the Space Net.

"Fire directly ahead!" Proton ordered, holding the control lever completely level.

Energy beams shot from his ship and smashed into the webbing of the giant Net, sending ripples toward all eighteen ships. His hope was that the weapons would burn a hole in the webbing big enough for him to fly through.

But it didn't work!

No hole appeared.

"We're going in!" Kincaid shouted.

Captain Proton barely had time to even grab for a support when suddenly his ship was trapped by the webbing and stopped dead in space.

He flew over the control panel and smashed into the wall.

Smoke filled the ship!

Fire broke out in three places!

Captain Proton tried to push himself to his feet, but just as he was about to stand part of the ceiling came crashing down.

A big part of the ceiling!

It smashed him to the deck.

And into blackness.

Chapter 9:
TROON FOR A DAY

Captain Proton came to as Buster Kincaid lifted the heavy ceiling panel off of him. The light was bright in his eyes and his head throbbed as if his heart was trying to pump all his blood out the top.

"You all right?" Kincaid asked, a worried expression covering his face.

Captain Proton rubbed the lump on the top of his head, then nodded slowly. "I'll be fine. How long was I out?"

"Only a few seconds," Kincaid answered.

Proton shoved himself to his feet and went quickly to the Imagizer. It showed they were wrapped in the Space Net and were being towed to a nearby planet.

Captain Proton ignored his headache and thought of their situation.

Things for them had never looked so bleak!

Constance had been kidnapped by the evil Queen Fems. They had been tossed beyond the reaches of their normal Galaxy to a place where they had been captured in a giant Space Net by unknown creatures.

Could it get worse? Captain Proton wondered. He didn't want to think about the answer.

With a thump their ship was lowered to what looked like a space docking area and the net lowered. Then there was a knock at the door to their spacecraft.

Kincaid looked startled as he glanced at Captain Proton. "What should we do?"

"Let them in, of course," Proton laughed. "What else can we do?"

Kincaid quickly went and opened the door, then stepped back as four very ugly creatures walked in. They were like no other creatures Captain Proton had ever seen before. They had spikes for feet, long arms with what looked to be clubs at the ends, and a large bag of some unknown substance stuck to their backs.

They looked as if they were constantly wet, with damp coverings over their heads and a slick plaid covering over most of their bodies.

"We are Troons," the leader exclaimed, his cracked lips flapping.

"Captain Proton of the Incorporated Planets Patrol."

"Yes," the Troon said. "We were

warned you were coming to take over our home, control our flags, destroy our greens in an unspeakable fashion."

"Why would Captain Proton do that?" Kincaid exclaimed. "He doesn't even know you!"

"Yes," the lead Troon spoke, his chapped lips flapping like loose flesh. He stepped closer to Captain Proton. "Why would you do that?"

"I would never do that!" Proton exclaimed.

"Then why did you come here?" the Troon puzzled.

"We were taken and thrown clear out of our Galaxy to here! We did not come here on purpose."

"But now you are here to control our flags, take over our home."

"Never!" Proton exclaimed.

"On that I agree," the Troon said. "We have stopped you so you cannot do such acts."

Captain Proton started to speak, then thought better of it. These Troons were talking in circles. Kincaid was clearly looking frustrated, so Captain Proton put up a hand to signal him to remain silent.

"You are charged with shooting at a Space Net," the Troon intoned. "Do you have a defense for such charges?"

"Self-defense!" Proton exclaimed. "We were trying to save ourselves."

"Why would you do that unless you came here to destroy our flags, take our homes, savage our greens?"

Captain Proton looked at the

Troon, then shook his head. Creatures all over the Galaxy were different. He had met evil ones and good ones, but never a race like the Troons.

"As I said," Proton explained, forcing himself to slow down. "We did not come here of our own free will. We do not want to harm you or take your flags

or your homes. We only want to go back to our home."

"Then why did you shoot at our Space Net?"

"Why did you try to catch us with your Space Net?" Proton fired the question right back at the Troon.

"To stop you from destroying our homes, taking our flags," the Troon repeated.

"And who warned you I wanted to do that?" Captain Proton demanded.

"Flog!" the Troon said. "Our blue god Flog warned us. Who else can see the future? We certainly cannot. He knew you were coming here. He was right. We assume the reason for your coming is also right."

"Blue?" Captain Proton asked. It had been a Blue Whirlpool that had brought them here. "Flog appears in a blue circle. Correct?"

"How do you know that?" Troon

demanded. "Only the Great Professionals of the Greens know of how Flog shows his vision."

"I am the greatest of all Great Professionals," Proton stated. "And I demand you take me to your Flog."

The Troons all seemed shocked. Then the one said, "You are not a Great Professional. You are Captain Proton who has come to take our flags."

"Ahhh," Proton replied. "But are you sure I am not Captain Proton the Great Professional, sent here by Flog to test you all?"

"We cannot be sure."

"But Flog will be sure," Proton observed. "Flog is always sure. Take me to Flog and he will tell you."

There was a slight moment of hesitation from the Troon and Captain Proton knew he had won the strange battle of words.

"Follow," the lead Troon intoned, then turned and left, followed by the other Troons.

"Why do you want to meet their god Flog?" Kincaid wondered aloud as the Troons left.

"He is the creature behind us being brought here," Proton answered. "And he can take us home. Now follow them."

"Oh," Kincaid muttered as he fell in behind the last Troon.

They were lead through the spaceport and into a giant building. What appeared to be grass covered the floor and mounds. The ceiling was far overhead and appeared to be painted to represent the Troon sky. Captain Proton could tell of no logical function for the structure.

They were led across this open green area to a large, blue lake. In the very center of the lake was a building, seemingly floating on the water.

"If you are a Great Professional," the first Troon stated, "you will know the way to the sacred building."

Captain Proton looked around quickly.

There were no boats, no signs of ramps to cover the distance across the water. Then he saw what he was looking for.

"Follow me," Captain Proton ordered, moving past the Troon to the edge of the lake and stepping directly out toward the building. His foot touched something solid just below the surface of the water. He couldn't see it, but he knew for certain it was there from the worn area on the grass leading down to the edge of the water. This test had been too easy.

The Troons let out a low *wow*ing sound.

Captain Proton walked directly toward the building, trying not to splash the inch of water he was walking in. Behind him he heard Kincaid mutter, "Amazing."

At the building he moved quickly inside and looked around. Under his feet he could feel the rumbling of great engines, but the room itself looked more like a simple control room than anything else.

And he had no idea how to operate these controls.

He quickly stepped aside and bowed slightly to the first Troon entering behind him. "I leave the honor of summoning the Great Flog to my hosts."

Proton moved over beside Kincaid and whispered. "Be ready! We're going through!"

Kincaid swallowed and nodded.

The Troon looked almost flustered, its chapped lips flapping without making a sound. Then it moved quickly to a panel and touched a big blue button.

The center of the room immediately filled with a swirling opening that had the same look as the one that Folke had used to enter their ship before the battle with the Comet Killers. Only this one was blue, the same color as Queen Fems' Cross-Galactic Door generated from her glass bracelet.

Captain Proton reacted instantly! "Now!" he shouted.

He grabbed Kincaid firmly by the arm, took two steps, and leaped at the blue swirling opening, pulling Kincaid with him.

They went through headfirst, side-by-side, before any of the Troon could even move.

More than likely he was taking the two of them to their deaths.

Around them the intense forces of the blue energy grabbed them, yanking Proton's hand free of Kincaid's arm.

Proton tumbled over and over and over in the blue nothingness.

He could see nothing, not even his own body.

There was no up.

There was no down.

And there was no exit.

It was all just blue.

Chapter 10:

ROTTEN TO THE CORE

The swirling blues of the Troons' portal to their god spun and tumbled Captain Proton like a sheet in a dryer, over and over, round and round.

Seemingly forever!

Yet oddly, he didn't feel the motion, didn't get dizzy, didn't become nauseated as he would have expected after such a long time tumbling and spinning.

He ignored what he thought he was seeing and concentrated on one thought: *Standing!*

There was no blue, no tumbling, no spinning.

Just *standing.*

Standing!

He repeated the word over and over until he realized he actually was standing on something hard. So he closed his eyes and willed himself to walk forward two steps.

Then he stopped and opened his eyes.

He was facing a large, round, fea-tureless ball of what looked to be white string, sitting on a large concrete platform. As he watched, the giant ball of string seemed to melt, forming a man with a long flowing white beard and white hair, wearing a white suit.

"Is this a better image for you, Captain Proton?" the man asked, smiling. His eyes were black, deep, like a dark pool of ink. The smile did not reach his eyes.

Around them the nothingness changed into a vast expanse of green grass, yellow sun in the sky, trees flowering with orange flowers, and birds chirping. Clearly as much an image made for him as the man with the white beard.

"Images make no difference to me," Proton replied. Then he glanced behind him at the circle of spinning and swirling blue hovering in the air. Kincaid had not followed him!

He reached his hand back inside the blue, grabbed a hold of Buster Kincaid's, arm and pulled.

Hard!

The ace reporter came stumbling out of the blue swirls. His face was white and he was breathing hard, but Captain Proton could tell his friend would be all right.

He turned back to the man with the white beard. "Would it be possible to be told where we are?" Proton asked.

The old man laughed, a cackling laugh like what might be expected from a witch in an old movie. "Humans. Always needing to know where they are. And when they are. Such small minds, never seeing the bigger picture."

"And don't forget who you are," Proton added, smiling back at the image of the white-bearded man.

Suddenly behind the man a spot of green appeared, swirling bigger and bigger until it matched the size of the swirling blue spot behind Captain Proton. Then Folke stepped through.

The man with the white beard and white suit immediately shoved Captain Proton aside and stood in front of the swirling blue, facing Folke in front of the swirling green circle.

Folke brushed off his black suit and smiled.

Captain Proton and Kincaid moved so they stood to one side, halfway between the two. It was clear to Proton that the two knew each other from the way they stared at each other intensely. There was no love to be lost between these two. And neither moved from in front of their swirling escape route.

"Well, Sandor," Folke said, smiling, "you have lured them here, now what?"

"Why are you here, Folke?" the one named Sandor demanded.

"Well, we have the answer to who you are," Proton stated, but both men with white hair ignored him.

"Neutral ground and you know it," Folke replied, still smiling. But Captain Proton could tell there was no real mirth behind the smile.

"What do you want with these humans?" Sandor demanded.

"Simply to give them a little truth," Folke replied.

Sandor turned to Captain Proton. "You believe what this entity tells you? Then you have smaller minds than even I thought."

"It seems," Proton replied, "that we are important to both of you. Would you mind explaining why?"

"It doesn't work that way, foolish human," Sandor snarled. Without even a glance at Folke he stepped into the blue swirling vortex and a moment later it vanished along with the blue sky, green grass, and chirping birds.

They were left standing on a small concretelike platform on what looked to be an airless moon. Yet they were breathing just fine, so Proton assumed something Folke was doing must be holding atmosphere for them.

"You sure made him angry," Kincaid laughed.

Proton shrugged and turned to Folke. "No chance of an explanation?"

Folke laughed. "As Sandor told you, it doesn't work that way, I'm afraid."

"So now what?" Proton asked, getting quickly annoyed at the games of these two beings.

"You continue onward, of course," Folke replied.

"We are standing on an airless moon, with no ship and no idea of where we are!" Proton outlined. "And you expect us to continue on?"

"Actually, I can tell you where you are," Folke intoned. "You are on what is called Core. It is the central point of all the Universe. From here all galaxies, all points in space are equidistant. It is the most powerful place in all of space."

"You said it was neutral territory," Proton observed. "Which I take it means your people and Sandor's people are fighting?"

Folke laughed. "We have stood on opposite sides of everything since the beginning of time. The yin and the yang, the good and the evil."

"The light and the darkness," Proton added. "But now I gather it is getting worse."

Again the fondness Captain Proton had seen before reached Folke's eyes.

"You understand more than you let on, Captain Proton."

With that, Folke nodded, turned, and stepped into his spinning green vortex.

A moment later it vanished.

If there could be a cold breeze on this airless moon called Core, Captain Proton was sure he felt it at that moment.

"Why'd he leave us?" Kincaid shouted, stepping toward where the green swirling circle had been a moment before.

"I suppose," Proton replied, "so we could find our own way."

"Our way where?" Kincaid demanded, waving his arm around the platform and the empty moonscape beyond.

Captain Proton knew exactly how his friend felt. The concrete platform they stood on was no larger than a good-sized bedroom floor, perfectly square, and seemingly sitting on a rock bluff on an airless moon.

"If this is the center of the universe," Kincaid observed, "I'd rather remain out in the boondocks."

Captain Proton moved to what he figured was the very center of the platform that was the very center of the entire Universe.

There he stood, feet slightly apart over that center, and looked around.

In all directions there was nothing but airless moon.

No stars above.

Only concrete below.

They were clearly trapped at the center of the Universe, pawns of two ancient races fighting battles that had started before Earth was even formed from space dust.

Kincaid moved over beside him. "What are we going to do? How are we going to get out of here?"

Proton looked out at the barren landscape without answering. There were no answers.

There were only questions.

And a long, slow death ahead of them.

Chapter 11:
HOME IS WHERE YOUR HEAD IS

A concrete-looking slab on a barren, airless moon was not what Captain Proton expected the center of the Universe to look like. He wasn't sure what he expected, but it certainly wasn't this.

Buster Kincaid sat cross-legged on the platform and seemed to be staring off into nothingness, which was all there was around them at the moment. Gray moon dust and black sky.

Captain Proton stood at the very center of both the platform and the Universe, trying to figure a way out, just as he always did in do-or-die situations. Usually he trusted his reflexes to rescue him, often his strength, sometimes his fighting skill. But this time, at this moment in his life's story, the answer wasn't in fists or movement, but in concentration and thought, his most powerful weapon.

And for what seemed to be the

longest time, he concentrated, standing there at the very center of everything. Now he thought he had the answer.

Proton moved away from the center of the platform to an edge. Slowly he stuck his hand out over the bare ground below.

Nothing!

No sense of barrier. No change in temperature.

He moved to the side where Folke's circle had appeared and stuck his hand off the edge again.

Again nothing!

"What are you doing?" Kincaid asked, watching him test the third side.

"Confirming assumptions," Captain Proton answered.

"And you were assuming what?" Kincaid demanded, moving over to stand beside Proton as he tested the fourth side of the concrete slab with the same results.

Still nothing happened when Proton stuck his hand over the fourth edge of the slab.

Proton turned and faced his companion. "I was assuming that what Folke told me was correct."

"And that was?" Kincaid wondered aloud.

"That this platform," Proton explained, "really is the very center of the Universe."

Kincaid looked puzzled. "So how does testing to see if anything is beyond the edge confirm that?"

"It doesn't. But by ruling out the possibility of it being something else, such as a transport station for those colored vortices, it helps the theory."

"And it's not a transport station?" Kincaid asked.

Proton shook his head. "No, but past that there are few tests I can try, so I must assume that Folke told us the truth as he saw it. This really is the center of the Universe."

"I'm getting a headache," Kincaid complained. "When you get it figured out, just explain it to me, would you?"

"Oh," Proton reassured his friend, "I have it figured out."

"You do?" Kincaid burst forth.

"This platform," Proton explained calmly, "is the center of the universe for Folke and Sandor and their people."

"You said that!" Kincaid exploded, very annoyed.

Proton went on calmly. "It has been the center of their fight for eons, if I understood them correctly."

"I heard that too!" Kincaid affirmed.

"It is a place they can meet on neutral ground."

"Okay," Kincaid followed, looking puzzled. "I know all that. But I thought you said you had it figured out about how we get off of this thing."

"Oh, I do," Proton answered calmly, ignoring his friend's pained expression.

"So when can we go?"

"We can leave at any time," Captain Proton explained.

"Okay," Kincaid snapped, holding up his hands in a gesture of surrender. "So why are we here?"

"I believe," Proton answered, looking around intently again, "that we are in a space outside our space, yet it lies over everything. Call it the space of thought, of dreams, of nightmares."

"I give up," Kincaid snarled and sat down. "I'm never going to understand."

"Are you hungry?" Proton asked.

Kincaid nodded. "Yes, it has been a while since I've eaten."

"You like apples?"

"Sure," Kincaid answered.

"Here," Proton laughed. "Have an apple." He tossed his surprised friend a juicy, red apple.

"Where did you get that?"

Proton held out his hand and another apple appeared. "I just simply thought of it being there. In a world of imagination, anything can be real."

"Profound," Kincaid snorted, sniffing at the apple.

"I thought so," Proton replied.

Then he turned and focused out over the barren moon around them.

Green grass appeared! Grass the green of Earth's grass.

And then blue skies! With a few fluffy, white clouds.

Trees, birds, and even a stream followed.

Kincaid looked stunned. "How did you do that?"

Captain Proton laughed. "I thought it was there, I believed it was there, and it was. Sandor did nothing I couldn't do in this strange space."

Proton stood, hands on hips, staring at the beautiful meadows and flowing blue water in the stream. "Actually, I think I have a better imagination than Sandor."

"Amazing," Kincaid muttered.

"Now, are you ready to go back to our space, where things at least seem real? We have a few challenges ahead of us, including rescuing Constance."

"Please!" Kincaid exclaimed, jumping to his feet and throwing the apple into the grass.

Captain Proton took a firm grasp of Kincaid's arm and stepped toward a yellow swirling vortex that had just formed near the edge of the platform.

"Where'd that come from?" Kincaid demanded.

Proton ignored his question.

Quickly he stepped into it without hesitation, only thinking of his destination and taking Kincaid with him.

Home.

His ship.

Earth.

For an instant the whirling took

his feet, but he forced himself to take two more firm steps!

Suddenly he found himself standing where he had expected to be standing, on his ship, next to his controls.

Kincaid was beside him.

Behind them the yellow swirling vortex vanished.

"Now I'm impressed," Kincaid exclaimed, looking around. "But we still have to get out of the Troon net and find a way to get across seventy years worth of travel to get home."

Proton moved to the Imagizer and turned it on. The scene that greeted him made him smile, even though it was expected. They were in Earth orbit, in the very center of the Incorporated Planets.

"How?" Kincaid muttered.

"This is the center of my Universe," Proton answered, pointing at the floor of the ship. "The minute Folke said that everything in the Universe was an equal distance from that platform I started to understand how we would get back here."

Kincaid tossed his arms into the air. "Lost me again."

"Everything in the Universe can not be the same distance from one point. Correct?" Proton quizzed.

"Of course."

"Yet Folke told us it was. Therefore, every place in the universe must be at that center."

"Not possible," Kincaid object-ed. "The entire universe was not on that concrete slab."

"Exactly," Proton beamed. "Therefore, every point in the Universe is a center. *The center* would be a better way of putting it. This is *the center* of my Universe. Since we were already on *the center*, I simply willed us to step to here. To my center."

"And the yellow vortex?" Kincaid asked. "How did you do that?"

Proton shrugged. "It seemed to be the most logical method of get-ting between points."

"Okay," Kincaid sighed. "I'm confused, but informed. Leave it at that. Can you take us anywhere with that yellow whirlpool?"

Proton laughed. "Nope. We're back to good old space travel."

He didn't want to tell his friend that even though they were home, Earth was in great danger.

"So now we go rescue Constance?" Kincaid asked.

Proton shook his head. "Not yet."

"And why not?" Kincaid asked, clearly not happy with Captain Proton's answer.

"Because my dear friend, we have a massive fleet of ships to recruit, worlds to convince to help us. There is a fight coming that we must win!"

"Fight?" Kincaid asked. "You mean between Folke's people and Sandor's people?"

"Actually, I doubt they have actu-ally fought in eons. They only let their pawns fight for them."

"And we're the pawns?" Kincaid asked.

Proton nodded. "Us and every other living being in the galaxy. This is the fight of light against darkness, good versus evil. We will win. We must!"

Kincaid sighed. "Fine, I'm glad you know all this, but can we eat first?"

Proton laughed. "Sure." He held out his hand. "Would you like an apple?"

Kincaid stumbled back, tripped over the edge of a control panel and sat down hard on the floor. "You can't still do that apple trick can you?"

Captain Proton broke out laughing, long and hard. "Don't I wish. Would make cooking a lot easier." He showed Kincaid that his hand was still empty.

"If it's all the same to you," Kincaid replied, standing. "I'm glad you can't do that anymore."

"I wish I still could," Proton answered, staring at the greens and blues and whites of the Earth on the Imagizer. "It would make this coming battle much easier to win."

"You think it's going to be that bad, huh?" Kincaid wondered.

"Worse," Captain Proton whispered. "Much, much worse."

Chapter 12:

SWARM WARNING

For two days after their return, Captain Proton talked to the leaders of the Incorporated Planets. He sent out messages to every civilized race he could think of, or that anyone had ever heard of. His message was always simple. "Stand ready. The fight to save the Galaxy approaches."

If any other human would have sent such a message, it would have been laughed away. But this message came from Captain Proton.

No one laughed!

All prepared for war!

On the morning of the third day after their return from Core, Captain Proton turned to Buster Kincaid. "Now it's time to rescue Constance!"

Kincaid shouted, "Yay!"

"Stand by engines!" Proton ordered.

"Engines standing by!" Kincaid answered, jumping to his position like an eager puppy.

"Full speed ahead!" Proton announced with one final glance at Earth in the Imagizer. He hoped to be back here soon.

"Do you have a plan on how to get into Queen Fems' Castle?" Kincaid asked as Earth shrank behind them, their rockets blasting them away at full thrust into the ether.

"I do!" Captain Proton answered, "but it may change by the time we get there."

"If you get there!"

Captain Proton drew his weapon and spun around to come face to face with Sandor, his blue swirling vortex behind him.

Captain Proton hated how Sandor and Folke could just come and go as they pleased. He kept his weapon ready and aimed at the man in the white suit.

Kincaid also had his weapon out and trained on Sandor.

Sandor looked at both of them, his long, flowing white beard and white hair appearing to blow slightly in an unseen wind.

"Are you planning on trying to stop us?" Proton demanded.

Sandor laughed his witch's laugh. "Of course not. I was impressed at how quickly you left Core. I wanted to come to warn you of a danger."

"You?" Proton asked, snarling. "Warn us?"

"Of course," Sandor smiled. "I am not what you think I am, Captain Proton."

"For the moment I'd rather not tell you what I think of you!" Captain Proton spit. "What danger are you talking about?"

"Ahead you will be ambushed by the dreaded Bugites of the planet called Red Mountain."

"Never heard of them!" Captain Proton scoffed.

"I know," Sandor agreed, again giving Captain Proton that sickly

smile and the black-eyed stare. "But they know of you and your messages of the last two days. They plan to stop you."

"And why are you telling me this?" Proton questioned.

Sandor smiled and Proton had a great desire to simply smash in the man's face, even though he knew the visage was an illusion.

"Just be warned," Sandor repeated, then turned and stepped back through the swirling blue circle that disappeared immediately after him.

"I really hate that guy!" Kincaid exclaimed.

"I wouldn't mind knocking him down a few notches myself," Proton replied, turning back to watch the Imagizer.

Suddenly Kincaid yelled, "He was right! Unknown fleet of ships dead ahead!"

Captain Proton could see them.

Hundreds of large, black, oval-shaped ships filled space in front of them. Each ship had a dozen landing pads sticking out on thin legs from under them and long weapons thrust out of the nose area. It gave them the appearance of giant black bugs floating among the stars. Captain Proton instantly felt loathing toward them, the same thing he felt about the bugs who crawled in the sewers or on the garbage heaps of Earth.

"Never seen anything like them before!" Kincaid exclaimed. "Down right ugly, if you ask me."

Proton stared at the screen, desperately trying to figure out any way around the massive bug fleet.

He couldn't see any way at all outside of fighting. And fighting didn't seem like such a good idea since they were outnumbered more than three hundred to one.

"Why did Sandor warn us?" Kincaid pondered.

Suddenly Captain Proton knew exactly how to get out of this mess.

He quickly picked up his microphone and stared into the camera mounted on his Imagizer. "Calling Bugite Captain."

Nothing.

He tried again. "Calling Bugite Captain. My name is Captain Proton."

"They are swarming around us," Kincaid shouted. "Should I arm our weapons?"

"No!" Proton ordered.

On the Imagizer the black bug-looking ships swarmed through the blackness, surrounding them.

"Why aren't we fighting?" Kincaid demanded. "We're going to die here if we don't fight!"

"Why should we fight?" Proton asked calmly.

"Because they are ambushing us?" Kincaid cried.

"Then it looks as if we're going to die without firing a shot," Captain Proton replied.

Kincaid staggered back, not believing what he had just heard Captain Proton say.

On the Imagizer, the black ships closed in like bugs swarming over a dead corpse.

Soon, it would be over.

Chapter 13:

BIRD OF A BIG FEATHER

The Bugite ships closed in like a swarm, working as a unit to close off any possible chance of escape.

Captain Proton watched as their black shapes filled the normally beautiful space with a sense of disgust, of loathing. He knew that much of that feeling was his own dislike of insects, but it was still hard to control. The Bugite ships just looked like giant beetles.

He calmed himself, forced himself to stand still and just watch. His greatest desire was to strike out, blast as many of their ugly shapes out of space as he could before they destroyed him.

But such action would not help save Earth. It would just get him and Kincaid killed.

"Should I shut down the engines?" Kincaid asked worriedly as he stared at the Imagizer.

"No!" Proton replied quickly. "We are on course and we will remain on course."

Kincaid shook his head in disbelief, but said nothing more.

Captain Proton knew that he had

done things before that Kincaid thought would get them killed for sure, only to discover the action had saved them. If he was wrong this time, they would be very quickly smashed under the heel of the Bugite fleet.

The Bugite ships swarmed around them, but none of them fired.

Captain Proton watched the intricate and complex motions of the ships first in disgust.

Then in wonder!

Then in complete awe at the ability of so many ships to pull off such difficult space maneuvers in such tight quarters, all while moving through space at a high rate of speed, pacing his ship.

"Captain!" Kincaid cried. "There is a tapping coming over the subatomic radio link."

"Amplify it!" Proton ordered.

A moment later the tapping echoed through the ship. It sounded as if someone was on the outside of the hull tapping against it with a hammer.

"Where's it coming from?" Kincaid wondered aloud, looking around the inside as if that might help him track the sound.

"It's from the Bugites," Proton replied, listening carefully to the taps at the same time. "It's a code."

"Do you understand it?"

Captain Proton nodded. "I do."

"What are they saying?" Kincaid demanded.

Captain Proton held up his hand

for Kincaid to be silent, then after a moment answered his friend. "They say that they are ready to stand with the Incorporated Planets and the Patrol in the coming fight!"

"Why don't they just come on the Imagizer and say that?"

"You really want to look into the face of a giant bug?" Proton asked.

"Ugh!" Kincaid grunted.

"I doubt they find us any more attractive," Proton suggested to his friend.

The tapping suddenly stopped.

"Give me a big wrench," Proton demanded. "Quickly!"

Kincaid dug into the tool box and quickly handed Captain Proton a big wrench. "Now turn the microphone on the subatomic radio way up so it catches all of this."

Kincaid did as he was told.

Proton moved over to a wall and began banging.

Quick bang. Quick bang.

Pause.

Quick bang.

Pause.

Quick bang.

Pause.

Long bang. Quick bang.

Pause.

On and on he went.

Finally, when he stopped Kincaid shut off the microphone and asked, "What did you tell them?"

"Thanks!" Proton replied.

"They're leaving," Kincaid exclaimed as the bug ships moved away in intricate patterns. "Where are they going?"

"To wait for the battle," Proton replied, tossing the wrench back in the tool box and going back to his controls. Kincaid bent to shove the tool box back out of the way under a panel.

"You were very smart," a soft voice intoned.

For the second time this trip Captain Proton swung around, blaster out of its holster and ready.

Kincaid came up fast, blaster also ready.

Folke stood in front of his green, swirling circle, smiling.

"I'm going to need to put a bell around your necks," Captain Proton snarled.

"You ever hear of knocking?" Kincaid snarled.

Folke laughed and ignored their comments. "How did you know you were not under attack by the Bugites?"

"Your buddy, Sandor, told me," Captain Proton replied calmly, going back to his controls.

"He warned you of an attack?" Folke repeated, clearly puzzled by the news.

"Exactly," Captain Proton sighed, turning to face Folke. "He warned me of an attack, so I did the opposite."

Folke laughed.

Captain Proton went on. "I was glad he warned me. Left alone, I just might have thought they were attacking."

Again Folke laughed the soft laugh that seemed to echo like a faint church bell on Sunday morn-

ing. "Sandor will never try that again with you."

"Too bad," Captain Proton said. "We could use all the help we can get."

"Of that"—Folke smiled,—"you are correct."

He turned and stepped through the green swirling circle. It disappeared behind him.

"Well good-bye to you, too," Kincaid snorted.

"Gods have few manners," Proton explained.

"We're almost to Queen Fems' planet," Kincaid declared.

Captain Proton stepped firmly to his controls and took over.

A few moments later they were skimming along the tops of the giant trees that filled the valleys around the Queen's Castle. He had decided they would land in the forest this time. The Queen's guards would never think to look for them in there, and the ship would be easy to hide.

A small meadow suddenly appeared below them and Captain Proton settled the ship on its jets directly between two monster trees.

"Engines shut off!" Kincaid declared.

"Are you ready?" Captain Proton asked his trusted friend.

"I just hope Constance is still alive," Kincaid stated, worried.

Captain Proton checked to make sure his gun was fully loaded, then he slapped it into its holster. "She will be!" he declared.

He swung the hatch to the ship open and glanced around, taking in the smell of the forest. A little damp, a little musty. A deep forest smell.

It was dark for midday, even in the clearing. Captain Proton studied the surrounding area carefully. Nothing seemed to be moving.

Kincaid came out and Captain Proton closed the door and secured it, making sure no one but he and Kincaid could get in again.

But before they could take one step away from the ship a massive screech filled the air around them.

Suddenly the sun was completely blacked out!

Captain Proton tried to spring sideways and draw his gun at the same time, but he was too late!

Far too late!

Faster than Captain Proton would have thought possible, giant claws wrapped around him, yanking him from the ground as if he weighed nothing.

A giant bird had him!

This bird was bigger than his ship, had claws bigger around than his waist, and a grip that was crushing his ribs. Its feathers were brown and light green, perfectly matching it with the trees and forest around them.

Proton forced himself to go limp and the bird eased its grip a little, but not enough to let him go. But just enough for him to free one arm and grab his ray gun.

He looked down. If he shot the bird and it dropped him, the fall hundreds of feet to the ground would surely kill him. Or if he shot the bird, it might smash him in its claws. Neither option sounded good.

He had no choice but to simply wait until the bird got to its destination.

Higher and higher they climbed!

Slowly at first, then faster as the bird circled up inside the meadow on what was clearly an updraft. For the last few hundred feet the bird seemed to never flap its giant wings.

Finally it soared out over the forest, miles up, making lazy circles in the air.

Captain Proton hung from the bird's giant talons, wondering what was going to be worse, being dropped or being eaten.

Either way, he didn't see much chance out of this mess.

In the distance, Queen Fems' Castle shone in the warm sunshine, mocking him.

So close, yet so far away.

And now he might never get the chance to rescue Constance.

49

Chapter 14:

OUT OF THE NEST AND INTO THE PAN

The giant bird circled over the forest for what seemed like a long time to Captain Proton. Where it had grabbed him around the chest hurt and he was sweating from the incredible heat coming up off the forest.

Then slowly the bird started down in giant lazy loops in the air. He tried to spot anything below that might give him a chance to shoot the bird and drop to safety, but even when getting close to the tops of the trees, he was still six or seven hundred feet in the air.

Shooting his transportation at this point would simply be suicide.

Then he saw where they were heading!

Covering the top of at least one tree was a giant bird's nest, big enough for four or five birds the size of the monster carrying him. There were already two there. And two others were circling above him, coming in, more than likely, for dinner.

And he had a sneaking hunch what was going to be the main course.

Fresh Captain Proton à la carte!

The closer he got, the bigger the nest looked. It actually covered the top of four different trees and was big enough to cover Patrol headquarters. It looked like it was made the same way an Earth bird would make a nest: with branches and feathers. Only these branches were the size of logs and the feathers the size of spaceships.

The bird dropped him about five feet above the nest floor in order to land.

Proton rolled on two giant feathers and ducked behind a log, working his way far enough into the space between the logs that made up the nest to stay out of the birds' way.

He held his gun at the ready. From the looks of the long, curing sharp beaks on these giant birds, there was no crack in this nest where he would be safe from them. If they started after him, he was going to have to fight.

Hanging under the bird coming in for a landing next was Buster Kincaid. Kincaid looked just as uncomfortable as Captain Proton had felt.

The bird dropped Kincaid from about six feet off the nest floor. Kincaid hit, rolled, and came up with his blaster in his hand, ready to roast a bird if he had to.

Proton stood, ready to back him up, but none of their feathered friends seemed interested.

Kincaid also ducked down behind a log much closer to the edge of the nest.

None of the birds seemed to be

paying them any attention at all, so Captain Proton moved from log to log, cover to cover, until he was beside Kincaid.

"Glad you made it!" Kincaid stated.

Proton patted his friend on the shoulder and replied, "Couldn't let you have all the fun."

Kincaid only snorted.

The two of them moved back away from the five birds now filling the middle of the giant nest like a herd of elephants grazing in a small meadow. Proton finally found a good hiding place even closer to the edge, where the logs were more piled up and there was more room down between them. If they had to, they could defend this location for a short time.

Behind them was an eight hundred foot drop to the forest floor. In front of them were battleship-sized giant birds with sharp beaks and claws that could crush a bus.

"So, any ideas?" Kincaid asked.

"Where are the guys with the swirling doors when you really need them?" Proton joked.

"I take that to mean no," Kincaid sighed, staring over the top of the log at the birds.

Captain Proton looked down through the logs below them, then over at the trunk of a nearby tree. The bark was very rough, which for giant trees meant that there was enough room for a man to get in the cracks between the bark.

Captain Proton studied the tree beside them, figuring it was similar to one of the ones holding them up. The fissures in the bark were like rock chimneys that climbers liked so much. They seemed to run from three to six feet wide and stretched all the way up and down the trees. It just might be possible for Kincaid and him to get in one of those giant cracks in the bark and lower themselves slowly all the way to the ground.

It would be a tough descent, but possible.

He looked back over the log at the birds. It was certainly a better choice than what faced them up there.

"I think I might have a way off of here," Proton declared.

"Tie some feathers together and parachute down?" Kincaid suggested.

Proton looked at the nearby feathers stuffed among the logs. "Good idea," he stated, "but I'm afraid we'd be dinner before we could get the chutes made."

"My thought exactly," Kincaid muttered. "What's your idea?"

Quickly Proton had them move over along the edge until they were close to being over the top of one of the giant trees. Still none of the birds was paying them any attention and Captain Proton could see why. He doubted any prey had ever escaped this nest. They could eat whatever they brought up here at their leisure.

After a short search he finally spotted a hold among the logs big enough for them to crawl down through and get against the top of the trunk of the tree. From there they might be able to lower themselves into one of the cracks in the bark.

Slowly they worked their way down through the logs, then Captain Proton eased himself over the edge of a branch and into a crack.

"Made it!" he shouted back up to Kincaid.

This high up the crack was shallow and fairly small, just barely big enough to fit his body inside. If he started sliding he was not going to be able to stop his fall easily since there was really no leverage.

He looked down. From what he could tell, the crack went all the way to the ground, growing slowly wider the farther down they went.

He arched his back against one side of the bark chimney and pressed his hands against the other, then lowered himself slowly. The surface of the bark was rough enough to give him good handholds.

He moved down six or seven feet, then told Kincaid what to do and braced himself solidly in case Kincaid slipped and he needed to grab him.

After a little hesitation, Kincaid

was in the crack above Captain Proton.

"Well, we're out of the nest," Proton commented, easing himself slowly but surely downward.

"I just hope it takes them some time to discover their dinner has taken a hike," Kincaid answered from over Proton's head.

For the first two hundred feet everything went as Captain Proton had hoped it might. They kept their backs pressed against one side of the crack while creating pressure with their hands and feet to lower themselves down.

At five hundred feet off the ground, Captain Proton found what looked like an opening into the center of the tree, carved out of the inside of the crack in the bark.

The hole, leading into a tunnel, was more than big enough for him to stand in and clearly wasn't something naturally found in the tree. Something or someone had carved it. But what would carve such a thing five hundred feet in the air? He had no idea.

He stepped just inside the hole and a moment later Kincaid dropped down beside him.

"Can you see where it leads?" Kincaid asked.

"No," Proton answered. "It seems to go in about five feet and then turn sharply to the right. Stay here. I'm going to try to look around the corner."

Kincaid nodded and Captain Proton eased into the darkness,

keeping his back against one side of the carved out tunnel in the monster tree. The light from the opening lit the tunnel for a short distance past him.

Suddenly behind Kincaid there was a loud squawk and a massive pounding of wings against the bark of the tree.

"Watch out!" Captain Proton shouted.

He could see exactly what was happening. One of the giant birds had landed on the side of the tree and was about to pluck Kincaid from the hole with its giant beak as if Kincaid were a worm in the ground.

Proton had his blaster out and fired past Kincaid.

The explosion of the gun echoed in the small tunnel.

He hit the bird directly above the beak, setting the feathers of its face on fire.

The bird reared back.

Kincaid dove farther into the carved tunnel and out of reach of the bird, his blaster in his hand.

Quickly he fired too, frying more feathers on the giant bird.

An instant later a very angry bird pecked its beak into the tunnel, sending both men around the corner and out of danger from being grabbed. If they had still been climbing down the outside of the tree they'd be bird food now. Their weapons had only made the birds angry.

Kincaid looked around. "Seems we're going to be here for a while!"

The bird tried to reach them again, the beak jamming on the corner, as if the tunnel had been designed to limit the bird's reach. For all Captain Proton knew, it had.

"We may be here longer than we want to be!" Proton stated, concerned.

Ahead in the tunnel there was a faint light.

Behind them the bird jammed its beak at them again. The smell of burning feathers reached them. That was one mad giant bird out there.

"Always wanted to see what the inside of one of these giant trees looked like," Captain Proton joked.

Kincaid didn't even have time to respond as suddenly the side of the tunnel smashed outward and pinned them both against the opposite wall.

Captain Proton tried to shove back, but the force was so strong, so fast, that he banged his head hard against the wood of the side of the tunnel.

The darkness took him quickly, before the pain set in.

Chapter 15:

CHILDREN OF THE GLASS

The light came back slowly to Captain Proton's eyes, followed by a dull, nagging headache from the pounding he'd taken.

Slowly he let himself open his eyes. Everything seemed blurry and distant. Even his breathing sounded far, far away.

For a moment he couldn't remember exactly where he was. His eyes cleared and he made himself stop and figure out that he was lying on his back and looking up. He could tell that much.

Above him towered the insides of a giant building, seeming to disappear into the distance. Light was filtering down through the giant space from long slitlike windows. Miles and miles of balconies and walkways lined the round insides of the stories-tall space.

Then suddenly he remembered he was inside a giant tree. Clearly a *hollow* giant tree!

He tried to push himself up to a sitting position, but the blackness threatened to come back, so he stayed still.

"Smart," a voice said from just to his left and above his head. "You really shouldn't move for a few more minutes."

A smiling face came into view over him. A face of a very small man who had to stand just to look down on Captain Proton's head.

A Nanoid!

But the Nanoid had no weapon and seemed interested in helping him.

Captain Proton eased himself up on one elbow and looked around.

He was lying on a wide, wooden balcony carved from the tree. From what he could see, the giant hollow room inside the tree went down as far as it went up. Every so often a Nanoid could be seen moving along a carved balcony.

Kincaid was beside him, also out cold, but still breathing. Neither one of them was bound and the one small Nanoid was the only person with them. Clearly they were not meant to be captives. At least that much was good news.

"He going to be all right?"

Proton asked, turning to face the Nanoid and motioning at Kincaid.

"Should have a headache like you," the Nanoid laughed a deep, rich laugh. "But he will survive. Our traps tend to do that. They knock you out but don't kill you."

"Effective," Proton granted, ignoring the pain in his head as best he could.

"Keeps unwanted visitors out of our homes," the Nanoid replied.

"We didn't mean to intrude," Proton apologized. "We were just trying to get away from those giant birds."

"We call them Dorcons," the Nanoid informed Captain Proton. "Big, dumb birds, but their eggs serve hundreds. Wonderful stuff."

"I'll bet," Proton replied as Kincaid moaned and slowly woke up.

Proton sat up and faced their

host. He was now looking down on the little man standing there.

"Captain Proton," the Nanoid spoke, "what brings you back to our planet?"

"You know of me?" Proton asked, surprised.

"Of course," the Nanoid answered, smiling. "We have agreed to fight with you and your allies in the upcoming great battle. We are preparing our ships now."

"Wonderful," Proton exclaimed.

"You have spaceships?" Kincaid asked, holding his head and tenderly feeling for a lump.

"Of course," the Nanoid replied. "You don't live in giant trees for centuries without learning what is in the sky above the tops."

"Logical," Kincaid nodded.

"To answer your question," Proton replied, "we have come to rescue our companion, Constance Goodheart, from the clutches of Queen Fems."

The Nanoid shook his head sadly. "You are too late, my friend," the Nanoid replied. "Queen Fems has taken your companion and left this planet. The Queen and the giants who choose to follow her have joined the side we will fight in the coming great battle."

"Do you know where they have gone?" Proton asked.

"To a place called Grayhawk Two," the Nanoid replied seriously.

The name made Captain Proton shudder. Grayhawk Two, the home of all evil in the Galaxy. The only

chance now to rescue Constance was to win the coming great battle between good and evil, between the forces of light and the forces of dark, between those that sided with Folke and those that sided with Sandor.

"Thank you," Proton said to the Nanoid. "Would it be possible for you to show us how to get to our ship?"

"With pleasure," the Nanoid replied. "But first there is one thing you need to see."

Captain Proton nodded and he and Kincaid slowly stood, making sure of their balance. Captain Proton didn't want either of them tumbling off one of the narrow walkways or balconies.

After they determined they were both sure on their feet, they followed the Nanoid to an open stairway and started down.

To Captain Proton, the little stairs were difficult, but manageable. As far as he was concerned, this was much better than climbing down the outside of the tree.

About two hundred feet lower they reached what the Nanoid said was ground level, but clearly the large hollow insides of the tree went down even farther.

"I assume these giant trees grew hollow?" Proton asked their guide about six flights of stairs under ground level.

"Of course," the Nanoid replied. "They have been here as long as time, as have we."

Captain Proton didn't have the needed moment to ask exactly what the Nanoid meant by that. The Nanoid led them onto a platform overlooking a giant underground space, formed by the intertwining of tree roots, not only from the tree they were in, but from other trees nearby.

From the looks of it the entire forest floor was simply a roof over these massive caverns.

As they moved out onto the platform a man in a robe with a long white beard turned and smiled at them. "Welcome."

Of all the people in all the universe, Folke was not the creature Captain Proton expected to see here. Clearly, however, their Nanoid guide was used to Folke.

"You again!" Kincaid snorted.

Captain Proton felt the same way, but said nothing. Instead he moved to the edge of the platform and looked around.

The giant cavern in front of them was covered with a white sand floor and seemed to go on forever in the distance, linked to other root-formed caverns. Thousands of sparkling colors seemed to be imbedded in the sand, but Captain Proton couldn't tell what caused the colors.

Nanoids and giant women moved slowly on walkways criss-crossing the sand, seemingly with purpose. Every so often one of them would stoop to check something. The women and the Nanoid

men didn't fight, but instead tended to help each other. Clearly not all the giant women had joined Queen Fems.

"I'm glad you found your way here, Captain Proton," Folke intoned. "It is better you understand the larger picture in this coming battle."

"Understand what?" Proton demanded, turning to face Folke. "I'm tired of all the games! Just explain it!"

Folke's eyes twinkled like the colors coming from the sand floors. He pointed to the sand floor. "See for yourself, but do not step in the sand. Stay to the walkways."

Captain Proton did as he was told, followed by Kincaid.

He went down and out onto the walkway over the edge of the sand floor. It took him a few steps to see what was causing the colors in the sand: large crystals similar to the one worn by Queen Fems and used to open her Cross-Galactic Door.

"Look closer," the Nanoid following them advised.

Captain Proton bent down and stared at one clear crystal stone resting on the white sand. This stone seemed to be sparkling green and red, and as he watched the most amazing thing appeared in the glass.

A child!

A Martian child, laughing, playing in front of a Martian home, the images clear in the crystal.

Captain Proton eased sideways

on the walkway until he was over a crystal sparkling with some green, a little red and a little blue. In this crystal Captain Proton saw the image of a small Jovian boy, playing with his pet Warkif.

Captain Proton stood and looked at the expanse of white sand leading off into the distance in all directions, broken only by roots from the giant trees. Then he remembered how massive the forests were on this planet. They covered almost everything except Queen Fems' Castle and the mountain it sat on.

"This is what you fight for, Captain Proton," Folke announced. "The children of the galaxy."

"What are these stones?" Proton wanted to know.

Folke shrugged. "Call them glass windows into the souls of children."

"And the colors coming from them?" Proton asked.

"The colors represent where the child is heading at this point in time," Folke answered. "If the coming battle is lost, the rainbow of colors coming from the children will be replaced by the blues of evil and the reds of anger and hate."

"As it should be," a voice said from behind them.

Proton turned to face Sandor.

Folke faced Sandor, but didn't touch him.

"You have lost, Proton," Sandor declared. He reached down and picked up a glowing green stone and looked at it with contempt.

"Soon this color will be erased from all the Galaxy."

He tossed the stone in the air behind his head, turned and disappeared back through his blue circle of whirling energy.

"The child!" the Nanoid screamed. "It will die if broken!"

Captain Proton reacted instantly!

He took three long, running strides down the walkway, then dove for the falling glass stone.

Somehow he had to catch it, or get between it and the hard walkway.

Time seemed to slow.

He wasn't going to make it.

The glass seemed outside his reach.

Just inches.

And because of those inches, a child was going to die.

Chapter 16:
BATTLE

In some fashion Captain Proton didn't fully understand, he managed to stretch out just enough to catch the falling glass gem.

Just barely enough!

It landed squarely in his palm and he protected it as he hit the walkway hard, bouncing and skidding to a stop.

"Amazing!" the Nanoid shouted.

"Well done!" Folke announced.

Proton sat up and looked into the

glass jewel he held. Inside he saw the image of a young Earth boy, sitting in a classroom staring intently at the teacher. Green and gold colors seemed to flow from the glass jewel, as if it were alive. If what Folke said was true, this kid was going to be a good kid  when he grew up, considering the colors flowing from the glass jewel.

If they won the coming battle!

He carefully handed the glass jewel back to the Nanoid, then stood and faced Folke. "It's time!"

Folke nodded. "The battle is being joined near Earth as we speak."

"We need to get to our ship!" Proton demanded.

The Nanoid put the glass jewel Proton had saved gently down in the sand, then announced, "Follow me. Our fleet will join you!"

"Thank you," Proton emoted. Then with one quick look around at the rainbow of colors coming from all the children in the glass stones, he followed the Nanoid up and to his ship.

Soon they were leaving orbit, headed at full speed for Earth.

Behind them the Nanoid fleet followed, thousands of small ships the size of a small room. But Captain Proton knew that those ships were very, very powerful.

The Nanoids were a very old race, and a race did not survive long in this Galaxy without being powerful.

"Look!" Kincaid shouted, pointing at the Imagizer.

Suddenly the Bugite fleet had joined in with the Nanoid fleet.

Then a moment later another fleet.

And then another and another.

"It seems like there's millions of ships behind us!" Kincaid exclaimed.

"There has to be," Proton replied calmly. "The fate of the Galaxy is at stake."

All the way to Earth they were joined by more and more fleets of ships. Some small, some numbering in the thousands.

Then finally, as Captain Proton led the fantastic combined fleet past Earth, the human fleet joined in.

Hundred and hundreds of different races fighting side-by-side. The forces of good were strong. Captain Proton just hoped the forces of evil weren't as strong.

But soon his hope vanished.

On the Imagizer a giant mass that seemed to fill all space between the stars grew in front of him.

Then slowly the mass separated into fleets of ships.

Hundreds and hundreds of fleets of ships, all following the large ship of Queen Fems.

Suddenly the Imagizer crackled and Queen Fems' face appeared.

"You stand no chance, Proton!" she stated, her gaze steely and cold.

"We fight for what is right!" Proton declared, flipping a switch to make sure his image was broadcast to all the ships. "And for the future!"

"The future you speak about belongs to those who have the power to take it!" Queen Fems growled.

"The future belongs to the children!" Proton countered. "We only defend their rights!"

She tossed back her head and laughed, then glared at him. "Get out of my way, Proton. You cannot stand against us!"

"I will die trying!" Proton declared.

With that she cut the connection.

For a moment all time seemed to stand still as millions of beings in thousands and thousands of ships seemed to hold their breaths, waiting.

Then one ship moved!

Queen Fems' ship fired the first shot!

"The fighting has started!" Kincaid shouted.

On the Imagizer thousands of ships swooped at each other.

Blue rays of death met green Destructo Beams!

Orange bolts of lightning fired against energy absorbing shields!

Red cutting swords cut at yellow flashes of heat weapons!

Ship against ship!

Race against Race!

Good against Evil!

The battle seemed to fill all of space around them.

Shots rocked Captain Proton's ship, but he ignored them. He only had one goal, one target: Queen Fems!

Explosions filled the void!

Smoke and destroyed ships spun like twisters on a Kansas wheat field.

The greatest battle of all the Galaxy was being fought!

There was no turning back now!

"Focus all our weapons on Queen Fems' ship!" Captain Proton ordered, yelling over the sound of destruction all around. "We will destroy the head of this evil monster!"

"I have her!" Kincaid exclaimed.

Proton powered his ship directly toward the Queen's ship.

"Fire!" he ordered.

Kincaid pressed the button and deadly rays shot from their ship, hitting the Queen's ship!

"Fire again!" Proton shouted.

Kincaid fired the weapons again.

Proton swooped his ship around the Queen's ship, ignoring all the shots they were being hit with. The ship around them rocked and shook.

One direct hit knocked Kincaid tumbling, but he scrambled quickly back to his post.

Captain Proton kept his focus completely on the war going on around him.

He dodged around one planet, coming in on Queen Fems from the side.

Suddenly a destroyed ship was in his way and he had to take evasive action. Then he was back on her tail!

Three of her ships attacked him! He ignored them!

"I don't know how many more hits we can take!" Kincaid shouted as again they took a direct hit.

Smoke poured out of almost every panel!

Sparks were flying everywhere!

"Fire again!" Proton ordered, steering his ship against the hardest barrage of fire right at the Queen's ship!

Again the beam of energy smashed into the Queen's ship!

Suddenly the Queen's ship turned.

Hesitated.

Then tried to escape!

All around Captain Proton saw the forces of darkness running scared.

The forces of light, of goodness were winning!

"Turn on the subatomic radio broadcaster so all ships hear me!" Proton ordered Kincaid.

"On!" Kincaid shouted.

"Your leader, Queen Fems is running!" Captain Proton stated. "Those of you who continue to follow her and fight will die! Stop fighting now and you will be allowed to return home!"

Suddenly what had been the greatest space battle of all time ended.

That quick and that simple!

No more shots were fired!

Ship after ship after ship, fleet after fleet stopped firing. The forces

of good reformed behind Captain Proton's ship, now far outnumbering the remaining ships on the other side.

Quickly, without being told to do so, the now leaderless fleets who had followed Queen Fems turned and left for home, separating into the wide regions of the Galaxy.

"We won!" Kincaid shouted, jumping up and down and up and down!

"I'm going after Queen Fems!" Proton told the entire fleet. "Tend to the wounded. I will return!"

With that he steered his ship through the debris of destroyed ships and into the void after the Queen's ship.

They had won the battle!

But unless the monster was destroyed completely, they hadn't won this war!

He was going to make sure that happened.

Or as he had said, he would die trying!

Chapter 17:

LOST AND FOUND

As Captain Proton steered his ship deftly through the blackness of space, Buster Kincaid did his best to fix everything that had been damaged in the Great Battle of the Galaxy, as Kincaid was calling it.

"I'm afraid," Kincaid worried,

"that we're not going to be back to full strength until we get back to Earth and have real mechanics look this all over."

"You've done a great job," Proton complimented. "Now stand ready. I think we're approaching the planet where Queen Fems is hiding. And I hope where she is holding Constance."

"Do you think the Queen is curling up in a cave, licking her wounds?" Kincaid chuckled softly.

"More than likely," Captain Proton corrected, "she's already planning her next attack. Evil never rests!"

"True," Kincaid acknowledged.

"Planet dead ahead!" Kincaid warned.

On the Imagizer an orange and red and blue planet swirled into view.

"Use the Energy Location Scanner," Proton ordered, "to locate where her ship is."

"Got it," Kincaid answered after only a moment of staring into the scope. "There's a big building beside her ship. It's on an island in the middle of a small ocean!"

Captain Proton quickly steered his ship down to a site near the Queen's ship.

"This island isn't big enough to hide our approach!" Proton observed as he shut off the ship and checked to make sure his weapon was loaded and secure.

"So we go directly in?" Kincaid asked.

"I go directly in," Proton corrected. "I want you to sneak around to the other side, behind them. They'll think I've come alone."

"Great plan!" Kincaid agreed.

Outside the ship, the air was hot and damp, like a summer day in Florida. Captain Proton's shirt instantly stuck to his back, but he didn't notice. He had much more important things to take care of.

Around them was junglelike brush and vine-covered trees. The Queen's ship was only a few hundred yards away, but those were going to be tough yards.

"Good luck," Kincaid whispered as he moved off to the right and disappeared into the brush.

Captain Proton waited a minute to give Kincaid time to travel the extra distance, then he started off directly for the Queen's ship.

It took him a good ten minutes to stomp and slither his way though the dense jungle before reaching  the clearing where the Queen's ship rested.

It was clearly damaged from the battle: black scorch marks all around and a small hole in one side. A large wooden building filled the far end of the clearing. Captain Proton could hear air conditioners laboring to cool the insides.

He started to step out into the clearing when a shot from an energy gun flashed past his face and destroyed a palm tree behind him!

Sizzle! Pop!

He dove and rolled, coming up firing!

One large woman fell with his first shot, dropping to the ground from the top of the building beside the ship.

His second shot cut down another hiding behind a large bush.

He waited for a moment, flat on the ground, his heart pounding in his ears from the close call!

Nothing!

He knew there had to be more guards somewhere. But the question was where?

He got up quickly and ran for the building.

No shot cut the air around him!

No sound except his own breathing filled the air!

He made it to the building and pressed his sweating back against it, scanning the surrounding area.

Still nothing!

He had expected far more than two guards.

He slowly eased his way around the building to the front door. Kincaid would be working his way toward the back door of the structure.

He checked his weapon to make sure it was still ready, then opened the door and dove through to the right, rolling on the hard concrete floor.

No one fired at him.

The building was empty!

He carefully studied the rafters and the walls. Nothing! Just concrete floor and nothing else. It looked as if the building had been used for some sort of farm storage sometime in the past.

The back door eased open and Kincaid glanced in.

"Come on in," Proton called. "Clearly we're at the wrong address."

"I heard shooting," Kincaid announced, clearly worried, heading for Captain Proton.

"Two guards outside," Proton replied.

"So where are the Queen and Constance?" Kincaid wondered aloud, looking around.

"Maybe still on her ship," Proton answered. "But that doesn't seem right. She came here for a reason and we just haven't discovered the reason yet."

They moved carefully outside and toward the ship. No more large women fired at them.

Nothing in the jungle seemed to be moving!

Nothing on the ship, either! The door was standing open.

Proton looked around, then pointed at the ground. "They went that way!"

He started off toward the nearby ocean beach, going down the hill. He had no idea what Queen Fems was up to, but he knew it would not be something he liked.

And for the first time, he was starting to worry about Constance's life. Up until the Queen was defeated, she had every reason to keep Constance alive and well. But now, she didn't!

The trail they had been following suddenly ended on the sandy beach of a large lagoon, divided from the ocean by a large reef.

Queen Fems and six guards were sitting in the shade under a grove of large palm trees about sixty feet up the beach from the lagoon.

Constance was tied up and standing in front of them, halfway to the water.

"Welcome, Captain Proton!" Queen Fems shouted down the beach. "You're just in time to see the end of your secretary, Constance Goodheart!"

Constance looked at him. She seemed to have been treated well, but now she was sweating and her dress was sticking to her. Plus her eyes were wide with fear.

None of the women, including the Queen seemed to have a weapon drawn. Captain Proton could see nothing that would be of danger to Constance.

Then suddenly out of the lagoon this giant creature surfaced, towering into the hot air!

The creature had huge red eyes that seemed to bug out of its head! It had giant tentacles that slithered and hissed along the sand and top of the water.

Two huge fangs stuck out of its saliva-dripping jaws as it reared up!

It was the ugliest creature Captain Proton had ever seen in all his travels across the Galaxy.

Constance screamed, the sound long and loud and carrying over the jungle.

Queen Fems applauded, clearly happy at the appearance of the monster.

"Cover the Queen and her troops!" Proton ordered Kincaid.

Kincaid did as he was told, pointing his gun at the Queen as Captain Proton ran for Constance.

But he was too late!

As he ran, the huge creature reached out with one giant tentacle, wrapped it around Constance's thin waist, and lifted her into the air!

Constance screamed!

Captain Proton ran as fast as he could, his weapon drawn!

The monster lifted her higher into the air!

She screamed again!

He wasn't going to make it! The sand was slowing him down! He was too far away!

She screamed again as the monster moved her toward its huge jaws.

And then again.

And again.

Chapter 18:

BUG-EYE THIS!

Queen Fems applauded as the Bug-Eyed Monster from the lagoon was about to eat Constance. Her guards cheered like fans at the Big Game! Brass bodices, short skirts, all they needed to make the picture complete would be pom-poms.

"Not so fast!" Proton shouted at the B.E.M., firing a shot into the side of the monster, aiming for the base of the tentacle that was holding Constance.

The Bug-Eyed Monster twitched, then paused, Constance just a foot away from its open, saliva-dripping jaws!

Constance tried to scream, but she was so afraid nothing came out.

As he ran toward the monster, Captain Proton fired again, this time holding the blast longer, again at the base of the tentacle holding Constance.

The monster twitched again, then shifted Constance to another tentacle, all the while holding her a good ten feet in the air!

The smell of cooking squid drifted in the air from his two shots. But it was going to take a lot more heat than his gun was capable of before this fish would be anything but sushi.

Proton ran right up under the monster!

The thing smelled of rot and evil!

No wonder Queen Fems liked it here!

The tentacle holding Constance moved her to one side and Captain Proton saw his opening!

He fired point blank right up past the monster's soft underbelly at the left, red bug-eye.

Pop!

The eye exploded like a dam bursting!

Red fluid sprayed out over the beach, covering Queen Fems and her handmaidens sitting on the sand.

They all screamed!

The fluid smelled like really, really sour milk.

The monster screamed, a loud, roaring noise that seemed to cut to Captain Proton's bones.

Now it was a One-Bug-Eyed Monster! An O.B.E.M.

But it still hadn't released Constance! She was swinging around in the air like she was on an out-of-control carnival ride.

Captain Proton quickly took careful aim to not hit his secretary, then fired again when his opening came.

Pop!

The second bug-eye exploded, sending more rotten-milk-smelling red fluid up the beach and over Queen Fems. Luckily both eye explosions missed him and Constance.

This time the No-Longer-Bug-Eyed Monster dropped Constance as its tentacles whipped around its face and empty eyes.

Captain Proton took two quick steps to the side and caught her!

Perfect catch! One arm under her legs, other arm under her back. Textbook hero catch of a falling damsel.

Quickly he backed away up the beach as the monster screamed and screamed and screamed!

Then slowly it retreated back into the depths of the lagoon.

Except for a few "Oh pews! Yucky! Ichey!" from Queen Fems and her guards, the beach was silent.

Captain Proton put Constance down with a quick hug, then turned to the red-smeared and very smelly Queen Fems.

"You will pay for this, Captain Proton!" she screamed, trying to wipe off the sticky eye-gunk.

Proton held his gun directly on her. "I don't think you have much to say about anything anymore, dear Queen."

She snorted, but had enough sense to not challenge him at the moment. She went back to trying to wipe off the smelly pink eye fluid.

Captain Proton had no idea what he was going to do with her and her six guards. Then the idea came to him!

He quickly motioned Kincaid to move up beside him, then whispered in the ace reporter's ear, "Go to the Queen's ship and without destroying it, make sure it will never fly again. Ever! Do it quickly and meet us at our ship!"

"Understood, Captain!" Kincaid whispered back, turning and running down the beach.

Proton now stared at the Queen. She smelled bad and the red fluid from the bug-eyes was starting to stick to her skin in the heat. It didn't look good on her at all, or on her dress, or hair.

"It is amazing to me," Proton observed. "How far evil can fall when pushed slightly."

Again the Queen only snorted and said nothing.

"Now," Proton announced, looking at the guard on the Queen's right. "Take your weapon and throw it into the center of the lagoon."

The woman did as she was told and returned to her place.

One at a time Captain Proton had all the Queen's guards toss their weapons into the lagoon with the blind monster.

"You all stay here until you see our ship leave," Proton ordered, making sure each of them, including the Queen heard him. "Then you are free to do as you please."

"You're not going to kill us?" the Queen demanded, a somewhat shocked look on her dirty face.

"Good and true people don't kill other people unless we have to," Captain Proton responded. "That's why we always win."

"You won this time, Proton!" the Queen snarled. "But there will be a next time."

"Of course," Captain Proton replied. "It just won't be against you."

He pointed at the lagoon. "I'd be careful trying to get your weapons back. That creature might have had a family down there. You just never know."

The Queen's guards all nodded in understanding.

He took Constance's hand and turned away from the fallen Queen, casually strolling up the beach. It was a beautiful island, he did have to admit that. The Queen just might enjoy her time here. He had seen worse prisons, that was for sure.

Fifteen minutes later they had made their way through the jungle and joined Kincaid in the ship.

"Blast off!" Proton ordered after the door was sealed.

The engines lifted them away from the island.

Proton, from low orbit, checked to make sure there was no other land close to the island, and no other races of people on this world. There wasn't.

The Queen and her six loyal guards were the only ones left.

Them and the blind Bug-Eyed Monster.

"You made sure her ship would never fly again?" Proton asked after they headed into deep space.

"It will never leave the ground," Kincaid replied. He held up a large square item. "This is its entire power source for starting their engines."

"Perfect!" Proton acknowledged.

"That's not all," Kincaid added. "I destroyed their communication equipment, the very core of their engine, and made sure their steering controls would never function again."

"Exactly as they deserve," Proton added.

"You think they'll survive there?" Kincaid asked.

"They have enough food, they have shelter, they will last as long as they want to. But without the Nanoids, they will never be able to have children."

"You mean the Nanoids and the Giant Women are mates?" Kincaid asked, clearly shocked.

Proton nodded. "Didn't you know that?"

"I don't think I want to think about that," Kincaid laughed.

"Good idea," Proton replied. "Some subjects are just better left unsaid."

"Oh," Kincaid added, changing that subject, "I also discovered while on her ship what the building was used for."

"What?" Proton asked, very curious.

"The monster must have been the Queen's pet. The building was used to store food for it. It's how she trained it to come up out of the lagoon to eat the people she wanted it to eat."

Captain Proton laughed. "When

it gets hungry, it's going to go looking, huh?"

Kincaid smiled. "Yeah."

"I hope she has enough sense to move to the other side of the island," Proton offered. Then for a moment both he and Kincaid and Constance laughed at the joke.

Then Kincaid observed, "I'm sure glad this is all over."

"Oh, it's not quite over yet," Proton warned.

"It's not?" Kincaid asked, sounding shocked.

"Not yet," Proton confirmed. "Just wait."

"How will I know when it's over?" Kincaid asked.

"Oh," Proton replied. "You'll know."

Chapter 19:

THE CHILDREN ARE SAFE

They were just over halfway back to Earth when the voice behind Captain Proton said, "You did well."

"Thank you, Folke," Captain Proton replied without turning from the controls.

Constance screamed.

"Doorbells?" Kincaid grumped. "Remember? A little warning would be nice to stop heart attacks."

"Don't worry, Constance," Captain Proton reassured. "He claims to be a friend."

"A friend who never knocks!" Kincaid snorted.

Folke laughed softly. Then faced Captain Proton. "Your dealing with Queen Fems was very decent."

"She didn't deserve such a nice prison," Pro-ton replied. "But it was the worst I could do."

Again Folke laughed.

"So why are you here this time?" Proton asked.

"Just to tell you the children of this galaxy are safe. For now."

"Good to know," Proton assured. "So Sandor is beaten?"

"I'm far from beaten, Proton!" the voice of Sandor came from behind where Proton faced Folke.

Again Constance screamed.

"I agree with you there," Proton snorted.

Kincaid held his chest. "I don't know how many more of these pop-in visits I can take."

Captain Proton took two steps back so he could see both Folke and Sandor. Sandor still had on his white suit, Folke his black one. Otherwise both looked similar with white hair and long, white beards. The colors of their clothes just seemed wrong to Proton, though, since Sandor was evil, Folke good. But who knew their reasons. Clearly they were something lost in the distant past.

"As the Queen said," Sandor

intoned, "you have won this battle, Captain Proton."

"But not the war," Folke added.

"Exactly," Sandor grinned.

"But without people such as me," Captain Proton pointed out, "and your good Queen Fems to take opposite sides, what fun would you two have?"

"True," Sandor replied, laughing. "I must find even greater evils to pit against the likes of you. Make it a fair contest."

"How about just leaving this Galaxy alone for a little while?" Proton asked.

Sandor broke out laughing, filling the ship with the chilling sound of evil. Finally he retorted. "The challenges against you, Captain Proton, have just begun."

With that the evil man in white turned and stepped through the blue swirling vortex that had appeared silently behind him.

Then he and it were gone.

Folke laughed softly. "I'm afraid he's right, Captain Proton. Evil never rests."

"Never hurts to ask," Proton laughed.

"Until next time," Folke nodded, turned and stepped through the swirling green vortex.

Proton looked at his wonderful friends, Buster Kincaid and Constance Goodheart. "It seems," he commented, "that we have work still to do."

Then he turned back to his controls.

Kincaid and Constance both stepped to their positions and for the first time in a while, the Galaxy

was back in balance and things felt right to Captain Proton.

They sped onward through the ether, ready to face any evil that would threaten the Galaxy!

THE PLANETS OF THE FUTURE

Mercury

THE PLANET MERCURY is perhaps the least understood world in our Solar System. Every schoolchild is intimately familiar with the Moon's crystal mountains and black seas, Mars' sandstorms and canals, Venus' steaming jungles and boiling oceans, Jupiter's Earth-sized hurricane and globe-spanning hydrogen ocean, even Saturn's rings and gaseous moons; but how many know about Mercury's quicksilver lakes? Schoolchildren the world 'round can describe the Moon's shy denizens, the stone-eaters of Mars, the green folk of Venus, the balloon-whales of Jupiter, even the needle-hawks of Saturn's moon Titan, but how many can tell you about the sandmen of Mercury?

Mercury's proximity to the Sun's killer rays has discouraged explorers until the recent discovery of Solaradium, which can be wrought into spacesuits to protect tender human flesh.

A Furnace World

IF YOU STEPPED OUT of your rocketship onto the glassy landing pad of a Mercurian spaceport—and if you weren't wearing a Solaradium spacesuit—the Sun would instantly blast you to pieces like a thousand ray-guns firing at once! The Sun dominates the sky of this tiny world, appearing many times larger than it does from Earth. During a solar storm, great streamers of atomic fire stretch out across the sky, chasing all offworlders into underground shelters. One word best sums up the memory of visiting this world: fire. Above all, fire.

The ground itself appears to have sustained millennia of atomic war . . . which, in a way, it has. The vast Northern Plains are one massive sheet of glass, sand melted over and over for billions of years, cooling as the year-long day passes into a year-long night, then heating and cracking again come morning. Fissures in the glass stretch for hundreds of miles, and this is where most of the Mercurians live.

Quicksilver is the name of Mercury's largest river, and this astounding travel route flows all the way around the world; quicksilver is also what flows through this river, for the only water on the planet is found in visiting human beings. Lakes jut off from the river every hundred or so miles, granting it a "lumpy" appearance from space, like a silver snake that swallowed a pack of rats. An observer on the shore watching the tall sailing ships can see a luminescent quicksilver mist rising from the liquid's surface to a height of a hundred feet before condensing and raining back upon the ground; this is how the lakes formed, and why all Mercury's beaches glisten magically. Tributary rivers stretch off into the north and south, a few reaching almost to the poles.

The Southern Plains contain one of the Hundred Mysteries of the Solar System: three thousand "Nickel Flowers." These amazing formations formed from nickel before the dawn of Mercurian civilization, and they are revered as holy sites. Each Flower rises a thousand feet above the glassy plains and looks mysteriously like an Earthly rose.  Impurities of scarlet iron run along the edges of the petals, tinging them with color so lifelike that early human explorers thought their rocketships' cameras had been mistakenly loaded with already exposed film that had photographed gardens on Earth! The sandmen believe that these metal mountains were built by their god Raggak, the personification of fire (and, some legends say, the Sun itself): When the world was young and without shape, goes the tale, Raggak reached down and scooped up great handfuls of liquid nickel. He turned his back to his fiery throne, the Sun, and pulled petals out of the cooling metal, then planted them into the ground where they could bloom in the rays of Raggak's glory. Human experts believe the Flowers to be artifacts of an as yet unknown alien race, possibly even mysterious space-ships. We will certainly be alert for news about these Flowers!

Glass Cities

THE NATIVES OF MERCURY call themselves "Kokkoki," but they are better known as "the sandmen of Mercury" or, more simply, "Mercurians." These incredible beings would actually freeze to death on a hot Earth-summer's day! They are even more energetic than the furious Martians, for their digestive system works like a blast furnace, separating important minerals from liquefied rock and storing pure silicon—powdery sand—beneath their stony skins the way humans store fat. They derive their energy from the ambient radiation of the Sun as well as from trace radioactives in the soil they eat. Luckily the sandmen are a peaceful lot, for if they had an inclination toward war, we would have little capacity to defend ourselves: A sandman, slightly taller than a man, weighs upward of thirty times as much as a human; his skin is impervious to almost any mobile artillery, and firing atomic weapons at him would only grant him strength; he can exist just as easily in the vacuum of space as in an atmosphere; he can lift objects ten times his weight and smash a fist through any armor short of a battle cruiser's; but most deadly is his atomic "scream," which a sandman uses to analyze the content of a stone (the way a shopper might squeeze a cantaloupe), but which could slaughter a platoon of humans. All this said, a sandman has never been known to raise a hand in anger against a human explorer, even before the first exchange of language and our subsequent friendly relations.

The sandmen's physiology forces them to live nomadically, typically moving from home to home once per season (much like a wealthy human doctor who maintains a winter cottage in Florida), so they always remain in the Sun's full glare. The sandmen are social beings, so it's not unusual to see millions of them living in the same square mile of crevasse. They build their cities in the miles-thick glass of the Northern Plains, deep enough so that their homes won't melt during the summer but shallow enough so that the sandmen can absorb plenty of sun through their clear ceilings. As shadows start to appear, the wealthier of the Mercurians move to their "afternoon homes," while the poorer migrate up from the lower (thus, darker) levels of the city to the abandoned areas. Some of the wealthiest mineral-baron sandmen own dozens of homes so that it is always noon where they live; the poorest slag-haulers who dwell in the cities' shadowy depths seldom move more than twice a year.

One architect sandman by the name of Chak creates fabulous glass spires during the Mercury nights. Working by atom-lamp, he and his dedicated artisans shape towers out of glass, some reaching hundreds of feet into the starry sky. Wealthy bohemians and patrons of the arts monitor Chak's progress and move into his architectural sculptures at once when they are complete, only to watch their crystal walls melt away at high noon.

Sandman Civilization

THE SANDMEN OF MERCURY are the most spiritual of all the Solar System's people. Everything in their lives centers around worship of the Sun-god Raggak. It's not difficult to understand why: Until only a hundred years ago, when an experimenter invented the atom-lamp, the Mercurians were entirely dependent upon the Sun for survival. Because their sole god has always been Raggak, and because Mercury is such a small world, the sandmen never broke into opposing camps; therefore, they are one in brotherhood, and do not understand the concept of war so prevalent among the Solar System's other species.

Wealth is derived primarily through mining and related industries. All the powerful families of Mercury can trace their ancestral wealth to the discovery of mines rich in atomic ores—this would correspond, in human terms, to a cross between a gold mine and a plantation. Young folk striving to make a name for themselves buy (or are given as a "passage-to-adulthood" present) mining equipment and go off into unworked territory, searching for the mother lode. It is said

that those in Raggak's favor will, if they work hard enough and follow their hearts, find where He planted rich deposits of ore beneath the planet's glass sheath. New fissures in the glass open up every day–year, exposing virgin land, so it is not unrealistic for anyone to believe he could be the next Mercurian Rockefeller.

A typical day in a sandman city involves extensive prayer (manifested by basking in the Sun on the surface, if possible—a reasonable ritual for these folks), followed by discussions about their democratic governmental processes, and a full measure of work. Even the wealthy must work, for it is Raggak's dictate that none shall shun labor. Of course, the rich find ways to keep busy without soiling their hands in the mines. While a solid third of the populace spends most of its life working as miners, nearly another third produces goods, and the final third provides services. A small number of sandmen call themselves priests, scientists, philosophers, or teachers.

Don't Miss Mercury!

Don't pass up the opportunity to visit this amazing world, but remember to be respectful of Raggak or you might not be invited to return. *"Haldag ot Raggak!"*

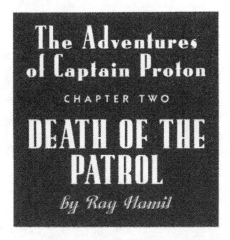

The Adventures of Captain Proton

CHAPTER TWO

DEATH OF THE PATROL

by Ray Hamil

In the last exciting episode of The Adventures of Captain Proton, *Dr. Chaotica's evil plan to take over the Galaxy would have succeeded if Captain Proton hadn't intercepted his dreaded Blaster Ship and stopped the runaway flaming red sun from destroying Earth. But to save Earth, Captain Proton dove his ship into a deadly Space Vortex from which nothing had ever escaped.*

Captain Proton's ship cut through the void of space with the swiftness of thought, the steering levers held under his strong hands with the control of a brain surgeon. They had been lucky to escape the deadly Space Vortex. He hated to think what might have happened if Buster Kincaid hadn't realized that their Imagizer beams could free them from the outer space vortex. He was just starting to relax when suddenly the entire ship jerked like a dog's leg in a bad dream and the world tilted sideways. Everything seemed to spin around Captain

Proton like a child's top on a hardwood floor.

Another smashing jerk shook the ship as Captain Proton fought to control the spinning craft. His hands flew over the levers. Yanking!

Pulling!

Pushing!

Pulling!

He worked the control levers faster and faster. A tiny bead of sweat broke out on his forehead, but he ignored it.

"Asteroid shower!" Ace Reporter Buster Kincaid shouted as the spinning tossed him from his chair as if he was a bail of hay falling out of a wagon. He rolled with a hard thump up against the base of the Super-Destructo Beam, Captain Proton's newest and best weapon to stop the scum of the Universe.

Constance Goodheart, Captain Proton's secretary, held onto a rail as something smashed into the ship. The ship tilted sideways and she screamed.

A second bead of sweat broke out on Captain Proton's forehead. He normally sweated when Constance Goodheart screamed, because when she screamed, they were usually in deep trouble. This time was no exception.

He shoved the control lever forward, then back. Then forward again.

The ship jerked and spun even more.

Constance screamed again.

"Imagizer!" he shouted.

Buster Kincaid crawled slowly to a large button on a panel near where he had been sitting.

"Hurry!" Captain Proton shouted, fighting the control stick like it was the head of a giant snake about to bite him.

Constance Goodheart screamed once more.

Another bead of sweat sprung into being on Captain Proton's forehead.

As the ship spun sideways again, Buster Kincaid hit the button, then smashed back into the wall like a rag doll tossed there by an angry child. This time space itself was that angry child. A very large, very powerful angry child.

In front of Captain Proton on the Imagizer the images of huge chunks of pitted rocks flashed past.

Constance Goodheart stared as a huge rock brushed past the ship, then screamed.

"We're doomed!" Buster Kincaid exclaimed over the roar of rough space. "There are too many of them!"

Another drop of sweat formed on Captain Proton's forehead as a massive asteroid grazed the ship, sending it spinning again like an out-of-control merry-go-round at a carnival. Captain Proton fought the levers, righting the ship, then shoved the steering lever hard to the right to just miss another huge asteroid.

Then, as quickly as it had started, they were through the asteroid shower and back into the wonderful relief of the emptiness of open space. Captain Proton took a long, deep breath and turned to face his crew. "Now, what were we talking about?" The beads of sweat on his forehead had disappeared.

Buster Kincaid climbed slowly to his feet, shaking his head. "I really hate asteroid showers," he muttered. "I wish the Patrol would map where they are."

Constance Goodheart slowly pried her fingers off the metal bar and smoothed her skirt, then made sure her hair was in place.

Captain Proton noted all of this, but said nothing. He knew, as a Captain of the ship and hero of the Incorporated Planets Patrol, that close calls were common in space. And the best way for him to handle it was as if it was an everyday occurrence. Often asteroid showers were.

"That last meteor just about smashed us to smithereens," Kincaid noted. "A few more inches and we would all be space junk floating out here."

Captain Proton shrugged. "We've had closer calls. Many actually." He didn't want to remind the intrepid reporter of their recent narrow escape from the Space Vortex after they had saved Earth from the flaming red sun.

Kincaid held up his hand. "Don't remind me."

"I wasn't going to," Captain Proton replied, smiling.

Suddenly the speaker crackled to life on the interplanetary vocalizer. "Captain Proton! Captain Proton! Come in."

"Must be Incorporated Planets Patrol headquarters," Proton explained, stepping smartly to his control board and pushing the blue button marked TALK.

"Captain Proton here," he explained, snapping to attention in front of the microphone.

"Return to Earth at once, as quickly as possible, and report to the Supreme Commander's office. Do you understand your orders?"

"I understand. Captain Proton over and out."

He turned around. "Kincaid, open the Atom Attractor screens and use the Sun to increase our speed to Earth. When we're within thirty-one thousand miles we will turn the Atom Attactor toward Jupiter to help us slow down."

"No one has ever tried that before!" Kincaid said, a worried look playing across his face. "We could die!"

"We're needed on Earth at once," Captain Proton replied calmly, yet firmly, hands on his hips. "You heard our orders. Using the Atom Attractor will save us five hours and sixteen minutes."

"Understood!" Kincaid shouted, jumping immediately to work at his control board, flipping switches.

"Atom Atractor screens open and aimed!" Kincaid reported.

"Attract!" Captain Proton ordered, then grabbed the control lever and held on. He knew no one had ever tried this before. He knew the ride was going to be rougher than going through the center of an asteroid shower and the Space Vortex combined. But he was needed on Earth at once and this was the quickest way to get there.

The ship shuddered as the surge pulled the ship toward Earth. Constance held on as the acceleration tried to shove her against the airlock door.

Kincaid grabbed the edge of the panel to brace himself.

The acceleration kept getting stronger and stronger. Constance slipped off her feet but held on, almost as if she were hanging from the bar. Buster Kincaid managed to stay on his feet at his panel, but not by much.

Captain Proton stood firmly planted as if his feet were glued to the deck as he fought to keep the ship lined up at the beautiful green planet ahead of them. Earth. His home. A dot of sweat appeared again on his forehead.

Constance Goodheart hung on, her eyes wide. But she was using all her strength just to hang on and had nothing left to even scream.

"Eighty thousand miles!" Kincaid shouted, reading off the dial in front of him.

"Seventy thousand!"

"Sixty thousand!"

Captain Proton fought the steering lever as if the ship were a bucking bronco. He had ridden bucking broncos before, breaking the steeds just as he could break any ship in the Patrol. His legs spread, his feet planted firmly on the deck, he fought the ship as it twisted, bucked, and tried to shake his perfect control.

"Fifty!" Kincaid counted, his voice getting louder and louder over the rumbling of the ship as the forces of nature and the Atom Attractor tried to tear it apart.

"Forty!"

"Thirty-five!"

"Turn the Atom Attractor!" Captain Proton ordered. "Focus it on Jupiter!"

Kincaid did as he had been told.

The ship lurched hard as the Atom Attractor beam suddenly cut off, then jerked back to life pulling  the ship in the other direction.

Constance screamed as she was flipped over the bar like a gymnast doing a giant swing.

Quickly the Atom Attractor slowed them.

Another dot of sweat formed on Captain Proton's brow, but he held on, keeping the ship flying true and straight toward the beautiful green hills of Earth.

"Perfect!" Kincaid reported as the ship finally swung into orbit.

Constance stood and applauded, even before straightening her hair and dress.

The dots of sweat on Captain Proton's forehead again vanished as if they had never been there.

A moment later they were entering Earth's atmosphere, completely under control.

Twenty minutes later Captain Proton and Buster Kincaid stood, arms behind their backs in a position of respect, facing the Supreme Commander of the Incorporated Planets Patrol.

The Supreme Commander's chamber was a massive room, with purple drapes hanging from the ceiling to the floor on all four walls. A huge table with a dozen chairs filled the center of the room. The Supreme Commander sat in the largest chair on one end of the table. Captain Proton and Buster Kincaid stood on the far end of the table, staring at their leader over the long expanse of polished wood.

"I have bad news," the Supreme Commander reported. "Dr. Chaotica has taken over most of the Incorporated Planets Patrol ships."

"How can that happen?" Kincaid asked, clearly shocked.

Captain Proton was shocked, also, but didn't show it. He knew how evil Dr. Chaotica was. And how brilliant. Such a feat was possible for such a man.

"We don't know," the Commander replied to Kincaid's question. "But we think it was with the use of his evil Mind-Sucker Ants. One look from a Mind-Sucker Ant and Dr. Chaotica controls your every move."

Captain Proton had heard of the evil Mind-Sucker Ants, but had always thought them a myth, much like the myth of the giant Flag Men of Troon.

"What will he do with the Patrol ships?" Kincaid worried.

"Easy answer, my friend," Captain Proton replied, "With the Patrol ships he can defend Planet X while he builds his Death Ray to attack Earth."

"Exactly!" the Supreme Commander exclaimed. "And I have to tell you the President of Earth is very concerned."

"Don't worry, sir," Captain Proton said firmly. "We'll save the Patrol."

"You are Earth's only hope," the Commander intoned.

"We will not fail," Proton reassured. He saluted and with Kincaid beside him they left the council chamber through a slit in the purple drapes.

Within the hour Captain Proton's ship was refueled and speeding away from Earth with Ace Reporter Buster Kincaid and Constance Goodheart standing beside Captain Proton staring into the Imagizer at the vastness of the Galaxy before them.

"How are we ever going to find the lost Patrol ships?" Kincaid asked.

"Easy, my dear friend," Captain Proton replied. "We know where they were when Dr. Chaotica stole them. We'll simply go there and trace them when we need to."

"How?" Kincaid asked, looking very confused.

"I will show you when the time comes," Proton said, laughing good-naturedly as if he had no care in the world. "But first we must make another stop."

"Where?" Kincaid asked.

"On the home world of the Mind-Sucker Ants."

Beside him, Constance Goodheart stifled a scream, then smiled at Captain Proton with a strained smile.

"Don't worry my dear," Proton assured. "I know you hate insects, spiders, and anything with more than two legs or three arms. But I will protect you."

She swallowed hard and then nodded as Captain Proton hit the Overdrive Jets and the ship surged forward into the blackness of space.

The Mind-Sucker Ants home world looked like a brown, pimple-covered lump floating in space. White-topped mountains thousand of miles high soared into space between deep valleys.

"I've never seen mountains like those," Kincaid exclaimed. "They're huge!"

"Of course you haven't," Proton snorted. "They're not mountains, they're ant hills. In the center of the largest we'll find the Queen of all the Mind-Sucker Ants."

"We're going in there?" Kincaid asked, his face as white as virgin snow in the year's first snow storm.

Constance made a choking sound, then seemed to slump like all the support had gone from her back.

Captain Proton ignored the reaction of his trusty team and aimed their ship right at the largest mountain.

"Hold on!" he shouted as the friction of the atmosphere lit the outer hull of the ship a bright red.

"Kincaid, fortify the Repeller Shields. We've run into thick air here."

Kincaid jumped to do what Proton had asked, punching the button on the board.

From out of the huge mountain ahead of them came a massive swarm of flying ants. Only these weren't normal ants. These were the size of a large man, with two legs and four arms and powerful wings supporting them. And the biggest, blackest, roundest eyes Captain Proton had ever seen.

Mind-Sucking Ant Creatures!

"There are millions of them!" Kincaid exclaimed.

Constance screamed, her eyes as wide as tea saucers.

Kincaid jumped to man the Destructo Beam station.

"No!" Proton shouted. "We don't harm any of them!"

"What?" Kincaid shouted. "We'll surely be destroyed!"

Captain Proton grabbed the microphone and flipped a switch. "We come in peace!" he said, his voice echoing over the land below as they sped toward the massive cloud of flying Mind-Sucking Ant Creatures.

The Ant Creatures all carried four Photon-Shooters in their four hands. Thousands of creatures times four Photon-Shooters each. No ship would stand a chance against such fire-power and Captain Proton knew it. But he pushed on.

He had to. He had to save the Incorporated Planets Patrol from the evil clutches of Dr. Chaotica and if that meant diving into a mountain high pile of Ants, than he would dive.

"They are ignoring you!" Kincaid shouted. "We're going to die!"

Constance screamed again.

"I'm going in the same hole they came out!" Proton shouted over the roar of millions of Ant-Creature wings as they surrounded the ship.

Kincaid looked stunned, then turned to Captain Proton. "They're not firing! How did you know?"

Captain Proton only shrugged.

Like a master seamstress threading a needle, Captain Proton managed to avoid all the flying Ant Creatures without hitting one and shoved the nose of the ship into the huge hole in the side of the white-tipped mountain.

Suddenly everything was dark.

Pitch dark.

Constance screamed.

Captain Proton understood her fear. Being in the dark in a cave filled with deadly Mind-Sucking Ant Creatures didn't please him much either. It was enough to give even a galactic hero like him the willies.

"Lights!" Proton ordered. "Not inside, but ahead."

Kincaid punched the button flooding the tunnel in front of them with massive high beams. The air was clear, but millions and millions of Mind-Sucking Ant Creatures filled the honey-combed walls, staring at them as they passed with huge, black eyes. Proton could feel their thoughts tickling at the edges of his mind, but none of them invaded his head. They would have been in for a fight if they had tried.

Constance took one look at the Imagizer and screamed. Then covered her eyes.

"Do you know where you are going?" Kincaid asked, gripping the rail as if he were falling.

"Down," Proton said, shoving the ship ahead around a corner in the tunnel and speeding onward.

Downward.

"Why do I feel as if we're going down to our own grave?" Kincaid mumbled, more to himself than to Captain Proton.

"A grave needs to be only six feet deep," Proton answered anyway. "At the moment we're over three miles deep and still going."

"Wonderful," Kincaid snorted, staring at the image of millions and millions of Ant Creatures covering the walls of the huge tunnel. "Their thoughts tickle."

Captain Proton laughed. "They do don't they?"

Somehow Constance managed to not scream again. But she kept her eyes covered tight.

At eighteen miles deep, the tunnel—which had gotten pretty narrow and twisting—suddenly  opened up into a massive room capable of holding a small moon in its space. A thousand spotlights all shown down at the center of the floor below, flooding the area as if it were daylight.

Captain Proton immediately stopped the ship and picked up the microphone. "I am Captain Proton of the Incorporated Planets Patrol. We come in peace."

"I know of you," a female voice said, seemingly from everywhere at once. It boomed, yet it wasn't loud. It was almost as if the voice had come from the inside of all their heads and been reflected off the walls and instruments of the ship. "Approach me, Captain Proton of the Incorporated Planets Patrol."

Captain Proton turned to Constance. "Don't scream when you see the Queen," he ordered. "She might take it as an insult and kill us all."

Constance swallowed, then nodded.

"I'm taking us down."

Slowly he maneuvered the ship toward the side of the massive space, lowering it on its jets slowly so that he didn't burn anything or any Ant Creature below him. Finally, after what seemed like an eternity, he had the ship on the rock surface and the jets shut off.

"Open the hatch!" Captain Proton shouted. "We're going out. Unarmed!"

"Unarmed?" Kincaid asked, clearly not happy with the thought.

"Unarmed," Proton repeated. "It's our only chance of getting the Ant Creatures to help us and getting out of here alive."

Kincaid pushed the button and with a mighty clang that echoed through the entire cavern, the door of Captain Proton's mighty Patrol ship lowered, forming a ramp.

With Captain Proton leading, Kincaid to his right, Constance to his left, they walked halfway down the ramp and stopped facing the mighty Queen of the Mind-Sucking Ant Creatures.

Captain Proton was very proud of his secretary for not screaming at the sight that greeted them. Flooded by the thousands of spotlights, the massive Queen's body was a mountain of white skin and blue veins. She was so large she easily would have covered all of New York City on Earth.

And she smelled fifty times worse than the sewers.

Captain Proton forced himself to not cough. Kincaid did cough. Constance only made a choking sound and then covered her mouth.

Thousands of Ant Creatures wearing no shoes and soft-looking robes climbed over the Queen's massive body like mountain climbers, washing, wiping, rubbing, patting, scratching. Every so often the flesh would move and one worker would lose his footing and slide off the mountain of skin and fat, landing on the hard ground of the chamber with a "Splat!" No other worker on the Queen's body seemed to notice and after a moment a clean-up team scurried out of a hole in the ground and picked up the body.

"Approach me," the female voice said, filling the chamber again and seemingly coming from everywhere.

"You two stay here on the ramp," he ordered.

"Thank you," Kincaid whispered softly.

Constance only choked back a faint sob.

Captain Proton strode forward off the ship's ramp and right toward the mountain of flesh. The closer he got, the bigger he realized she was. And the worse she smelled.

Her head, if it was on the top of that mountain, had to be a thousand feet in the air. He also noticed for the first time a large line of Ant Creatures with baskets of food on their shoulders streaming toward the Queen, climbing upward steadily, pouring their food into a massive hole in the side of the flesh, and then going back down. Clearly thousands and thousands kept her fed continuously. But if she was the mother to this entire race, it made sense.

"Stop!" the Queen said.

Captain Proton stopped instantly and stood at attention, staring upward at where he guessed the Queen's head and eyes were.

"I know you are here to ask for my help," the Queen intoned, her words massive and filling.

"Yes, your Highness, I am."

"I will grant you that help," she said. "Dr. Chaotica used my people and my ships against my will to capture your Patrol Fleet. I will not stand for that."

With that sentence the entire mountain of flesh shook with what appeared to be waves of anger. Hundreds of workers on the Queen's body slipped and fell to

their deaths in a massive, rapid-fire *Splat! Splat! Splat!*

Clearly the Queen was not happy with Dr. Chaotica.

"Thank you, Great Queen. With your help, we will defeat Dr. Chaotica."

"Go now," she ordered. "Before my next birthing cycle starts and floods this chamber with my young."

Captain Proton glanced around at the massive, moon-sized room and almost shuddered at the thought of that many baby Mind-Sucking Ant Creatures filling it.

"Thank you," he replied, bowed and turned for his ship.

When he reached the bottom of the ramp Constance and Kincaid both turned and went back inside. Kincaid's face was white. Constance looked as if she was going to be sick at any moment.

"Well done, crew," Proton complimented as the door slammed shut and they lifted off.

Ten minutes later he had maneuvered the ship back out of the long tunnel and into space, where a massive fleet of Ant-Creature Warships waited.

Captain Proton took his ship right up to the edge of the war fleet, paused for a moment to show respect to the commander of those ships, then turned and headed off into space toward the last known position of the Patrol ships the evil Dr. Chaotica had captured.

"They're following," Kincaid said. "Thousands of them."

Proton only nodded. He had known they would.

"Good luck," the Queen said, her voice filling the ship as if she were speaking from every panel, every wall.

"Thank you," Captain Proton answered aloud, never taking his eyes off the Imagizer showing empty space ahead.

For the next few hours none of them said a word. It was just better that way.

H ow are we going to find out where Dr. Chaotica has taken the Patrol ships?" Kincaid asked as Captain Proton slowed their ship to a stop in space at the very point where Dr. Chaotica had taken them. The thousands of Mind-Sucking Ant Creature warships behind them also slowed and stopped, waiting.

"Easy," Proton answered laughingly. "We'll track them."

"How?" Kincaid asked, looking puzzled. "There's nothing out there but the blackness of space, the cold of nothingness, the emptiness of the void."

"I know," Captain Proton chortled.

"Then how?" Kincaid asked, clearly getting a little frustrated.

"Simple, actually," Captain Proton replied. He went over to a wall and tapped in three places in a precise order. A super-secret panel opened and he reached inside and pulled out what looked like a large flashlight.

"I didn't know that was there," Kincaid said, pointing at the super-secret panel.

"No one but me and the President of Earth knew it was there," Captain Proton said, looking very serious. "And if it had been opened by anyone but me, it would have exploded and destroyed the ship."

"Oh," Kincaid sighed.

Captain Proton stood there seriously, making sure his point was made.

"What is that?" Kincaid asked, pointing at the flashlight-looking device.

Proton held up the device, which seemed light in his powerful hands. But light didn't mean it wasn't important. It was. Actually it was very important, and only one of two in the entire Galaxy. "It's a Tratanium Reactionary Atomic Coordinating Kaleidoscope Energy Reducer."

Kincaid looked puzzled.

Proton laughed. "Just call it a T.R.A.C.K.E.R. for short, which is actually what it does." He handed it to Kincaid. "Replace the Energizing Coil in our Space Lights with this."

Kincaid carefully took the T.R.A.C.K.E.R. and opened a panel on his control board and put it inside.

"Ready?" Captain Proton asked.

"Ready, Captain," Kincaid replied.

"Imagizer on!"

"On, Captain," Kincaid replied.

"Space Lights on!" Captain Proton ordered.

"On, Captain," Kincaid assured.

On the Imagizer the most astonishing sight appeared. Where once had been simply open, cold, empty, space now suddenly there were bright purple lines heading off into the depths of space.

Constance gasped.

"Patrol ships all leave a trail," Captain Proton stated.

"When looked at through a T.R.A.C.K.E.R." Kincaid said. "No wonder it is so super-secret."

"Exactly," Captain Proton said. "Now it's time we go get our ships back, don't you think?"

"Ready when you are," Kincaid replied, smiling.

Captain Proton hit the Jets and turned his ship to follow the purple lines in space.

Behind him thousands of Mind-Sucking Ant Creature Warships followed.

The purple lines in space, left by the Patrol ships after being captured by Dr. Chaotica, led directly toward the Great Comet Storm in the outer system. The Great Comet Storm is a mass of hundreds of comets, all traveling through space together, sometimes side by side, other times trailing each other in long lines, their beautiful tails spread out like fans behind them.

"They sure are beautiful," Kincaid said, clearly awed.

Constance stood, staring, her mouth open.

"They sure are," Captain Proton

agreed. "Space can be a very beautiful place, there is no doubt. And very deadly." He pointed to the sixth comet in a line of ten. The purple trails left by the Patrol ships all headed there.

"To a comet?" Kincaid said.

"Makes as much sense as anywhere else," Proton stated. "Miss Goodheart, brace yourself. Kincaid, take your station. We're going in."

Kincaid stepped firmly to his station. Constance grabbed a railing.

Captain Proton thrust the ship forward directly at the hurtling comet. Behind him, he noted, the thousands of Mind-Sucking Ant-Creature Warships fanned out into attack formation a distance back.

It took only a moment before their ship burst through the first layer of dust over the comet and saw what was happening below. Dr. Chaotica had created a massive factory to refit all the Patrol ships he had captured. Most of the head of the comet was covered in Patrol ships. And hundreds of Dr. Chaotica's fleet faced them.

Dr. Chaotica's evil laughing face filled the screen. "Captain Proton! I thought I had finished you in the Space Vortex!"

"You will discover, Chaotica," Proton answered calmly, "that I do not die easily!"

Chaotica threw back his head and laughed. Then he spoke clearly into his microphone, "But you will die today. Your one ship against my fleet. You stand no chance!"

"I think you need to see what's coming through the comet's dust cloud behind me," Proton said.

Dr. Chaotica glanced to his right, then turned back to face Proton. He was not laughing. "We will see who is the master today, Proton!" Chaotica sneered. "And who will be the master of the Galaxy." With that he cut the connection.

"He didn't like the looks of our friends, I guess," Kincaid chuckled.

"Not many people would," Proton agreed.

"Chaotica's ships are getting ready to fire!" Kincaid observed.

Constance screamed.

"Don't return fire until I give the order!" Proton shouted.

A moment later the lightning-shaped beams of Dr. Chaotica's weapons lashed out at them and the Mind-Sucking Ant-Creature Warships now coming through the comet's dust behind them.

The ship rocked, but Proton kept his course, blasting ahead.

Constance screamed.

Kincaid braced himself. "Now?"

"Not yet!" Proton shouted. "We don't want to take any chances of hitting our own ships!"

"Good thinking!" Kincaid agreed.

Again Dr. Chaotica's beams rocked the ship.

"We've been hit!" Kincaid shouted.

"Fire the Destructo Beam!" Proton ordered.

Kincaid punched the button on his panel and instantly one of Dr. Chaotica's ships exploded in a bright flash of light and thunder.

"Got him!" Kincaid exclaimed.

"Great shooting!" Captain Proton agreed.

Around them the scene became something out of a nightmare. Thousands of Mind-Sucking Ant-Creature Warships opened fire, their beams snaking out like black whips, snapping around Dr. Chaotica's ships, sending them spinning away.

After only a moment it was clear that the Mind-Sucking Ant-Creature's weapons were stronger than Dr. Chaotica's weapons. Captain Proton was very glad the Ants were on his side.

"Find Dr. Chaotica's personal ship!" Captain Proton ordered. Both he and Kincaid knew exactly what it looked like, since they had seen it just before being sucked down into the Space Vortex.

"There it is!" Kincaid shouted as another blast from a Chaotica ship rocked them. "He's trying to get away through the comet's tail."

Proton only nodded.

"He'll be destroyed," Kincaid laughed. "No ship has ever made it through a comet's tail and lived to tell the tale."

Captain Proton gave his trusted friend a frown, then turned back to his controls. "The Ant Creatures can take care of the rest of Dr. Chaotica's ships."

"Easily," Kincaid agreed.

"The Patrol ships are rescued and again Earth is saved."

"There will be cheering in the streets of Earth today," Kincaid agreed again, smiling.

"Yes, there will," Captain Proton observed, frowning as he stared ahead. "But we have one more thing to do before we can join such a celebration."

"What's that?" Kincaid asked.

"We're going after Dr. Chaotica!" Constance screamed.

"Into the tail of a comet?" Kincaid exclaimed. "He won't survive in there. We don't need to go after him."

"Yes we do," Captain Proton replied firmly. "In case he survives. He must be stopped."

"But in the tail of a comet?" Kincaid asked.

"Yes," Captain Proton answered firmly. He picked up the microphone and spoke sternly. "Ant Creatures. Continue the fight. I will go after the leader, Dr. Chaotica. And if we do not return, I want to say one thing. Earth thanks you."

Kincaid looked pale as Captain Proton glanced back at him. "Ready?"

Kincaid only nodded.

Captain Proton braced his feet and thrust the control lever forward, sending them behind the comet and into its tail.

Almost instantly they lost sight of the battle still being fought.

"Replace the T.R.A.C.K.E.R. in the light system with a High Beam Magnifier!" Captain Proton ordered. "We need lights!"

Kincaid jumped to do as Captain Proton had ordered, but he was just a fraction too late.

"You dare follow me into the grasp of hell, Proton?" Dr. Chaotica's evil voice echoed. "You are a brave man. Too bad you have to die!"

Dr. Chaotica's evil laugh was cut off with a blast that seemed to light up the comet dust around them.

Their ship twisted end-over-end as Captain Proton fought to bring it under control.

Constance screamed.

Kincaid was tossed against the base of the Destructo Beam.

"Get the lights on!" Captain Proton shouted as he fought the control lever.

Kincaid crawled back over to the panel and snapped on the lights, showing them what was outside.

Again Constance screamed.

"We're going into the mouth of the Giant Comet!" Kincaid shouted.

Proton said nothing as he fought to regain control, sweat pouring off his forehead like he was standing in a shower.

"The ship is not coming around!" Kincaid shouted.

"The forces of the Giant Comet have us in its death grip!" Captain Proton shouted, fighting the lever as the ship spun.

And spun.

And spun.

Downward.

Downward.

Downward.

And as the ship vanished into the mouth of the Giant Comet, the sounds of Dr. Chaotica's laughter could be heard throughout the Galaxy. Laughter that sent shivers down the backs of every good citizen. For without Captain Proton, no one was safe.

To be continued . . .

THE CITY OF THE FUTURE

JOURNEY ACROSS the fifth dimension to the year 2000 and watch as Captain Proton traverses the world, hot on the heels of a super-villain:

Seattle of the Year 2000

SCIENTISTS HAVE USED futuristic technology to reform once-dreary Seattle into a year-round vacation destination now known as "the jewel of the Northwest." A great scaffold rises from the surrounding foothills like a mighty hand, reaching megallanium-alloy fingers into the stratosphere, and extending across Elliot Bay to the Olympic Peninsula. Even today, government scientists are hard at work creating such materials. This alloy is so strong that the engineers who designed the "Paradise Dome" were able to make its beams so thin that one can only see them from downtown Seattle using a triocular. Perhaps more amazing, a tourist flyer says that this incredible structure weighs less than the razed Empire State Building! Remember, the scientists and engineers of the future are students today, so lend a youngster a hand; he may invent megallanium tomorrow.

Within the diamond-shaped latticework of the Dome, millions of microscopic weather stators hum quietly to themselves as they emit their controlling rays into the sky. Molecule-sized fusion reactors at every scaffolding intersection power these devices, absorbing hydrogen from the atmosphere and turning it into electricity for the stators as well as for the city below. A panel of climate and crop experts carefully plan each year's weather well in advance, commanding rain when needed—usually during the early morning when few people will be inconvenienced by it, and also cleansing the air for folks before they go off to work—or summer clouds to help moderate a hot day.

Today, for instance, the winter sky overhead is clear and crisp, men and women dress in light coats, the sun is a warming disk against a blue backdrop . . . even while clouds roil at the horizons, endlessly dumping millions of gallons of rain upon regions unfortunately beyond the Dome's influence. Sorry, Olympia! Only a decade ago, Seattleites used to endure half a year of gloom, and no one but sailors would live here, which is what prompted the city fathers to implement this superscience. Now millions of professional men and women from around the globe choose Seattle as their home, and high-tech businesses have selected this once-sodden locale as

their base—something that would never have happened if they had to worry about months of morale-crushing darkness and washed-out roads.

Fresh air passes through the scaffold as through a screen door, but the weather-stators' rays also help calm the bluster of winter storms, rendering a gale wind into a refreshing breeze.

But what is most astounding about this great Dome is that it is not the only one! Many cities possess such Domes: London (though that one is also reinforced with radar-cannon to serve as a shield against air-raids), New York City (including Manhattan), and Mexico City are among the two dozen international cities that have built such impressive tools for the comfort and productivity of their citizens. The Reds in Moscow say the Domes are "cradles for lazy capitalists," but rumor has it they are developing a satellite capable of controlling the weather of their entire continent! The Chinese are said to be alarmed by this possibility. Stay tuned.

Homes in the Year 2000

THE YOUNG FAMILY of tomorrow has many more housing options than we do. Great apartment spires rise from the park like downtown city blocks like mile-high sequoias, each tower housing as many as ten thousand people. The central elevator cylinder houses four glass-walled, pie-shaped elevators that automatically identify who steps aboard and whisks them silently to their front door in seconds; these shoot up and down on a cushion of nitrogen below, and they are sealed from the vacuum above by electromagnetics. This pneumatic system also helps preserve the building from fire, since nothing can burn without oxygen. In case of fire, the residents in the year 2000 *always* use elevators for safe escapes!

Each apartment unit is more like a house cantilevered from the central cylinder. People sometimes buy these apartments—but most commonly, they purchase linear footage along the outside of the cylinder, and then build entire homes suspended in midair as large as any mansion of our day, but with a view that would astound even those living on mountainsides. The smaller homes and apartments look much like boxes hung from one side of the shaft, but the larger ones completely encircle the cylinder like giant Life Savers.

Some of these spires reach all the way to the Dome, helping suspend it while adding rigidity to these needle-thin buildings themselves.

Naturally, many people still live in traditional homes or apartments, but Seattle walks on the forefront of domestic technology, and the residents plan to eliminate all ground clutter within the next decade.

Communication in the Year 2000

NO LONGER MUST people wait for the delivery boy to drop off their morning paper in order to read the news. All across Seattle, on every streetcorner, one finds the ubiquitous public viewplate. Local companies donate these telephone-booth-sized devices out of human benevolence and civic pride, a shining example of how the corporations of the future have grown more community-oriented; of course, the donating company's name is stenciled on the rear of each machine. Atop the box of the newsvisor glows a neon number, indicating to which of ten news stations (1-2 cover local news, 3-5 national, 6-8 international, and 7-10 Solar System) the machine is tuned. These also serve as emergency booths: If one is in need of police, fire, or medical assistance, all any good neighbor need do is throw the appropriate lever on the side of the newsvisor and emergency workers will appear within minutes. These, like all public services, run on electricity generated by the Dome's miniature reactors.

However, Seattleites usually need not search for a newsvisor if they need to place a call. All Americans (and, in the year 2000, people who once considered themselves Canadians now proudly call themselves Americans, as well—except for former province Quebec, which now calls itself the nation of Canada) wear teleradio sets. Men normally wear the miniature boxes on their wrists, since they serve double-duty as wristwatches; while women normally wear more aesthetically designed sets in the form of pearlescent pendants or polished hairclips. These teleradios perform all the functions of present-day telephones, yet also work like radios in that the user can place a call to a colleague aboard an airplane or even a family member living on the Moon! One Seattle company makes a special teleradio that acts as a message-recorder, a daily meeting-calendar, and an automatic letter-writer, but it is not very popular as most people will never entrust electronic brains with managing their careers.

Transportation in the Year 2000

LIKE MOST PEOPLE, Captain Proton rides the free civic trolley. Every First-World city operates two air-trolleys per major street, and several run twenty-four hours a day. Gone are the days of gridlock now that urban dwellers have forsaken their commuter automobiles. Employees arrive at their work-places on time every day and spend much less time getting to and from work and home, since the air-trolleys possess exclusive access to the first-level air lane above the anti-quated roads. Delivery vehicles may still cling to the pavement and creep to their destinations at forty miles-per-hour in town, but air-trolleys whoosh from block to block in seconds, stopping at raised plat-forms to drop off and collect pas-sengers. The flat-bottomed, spher-oid air-trolleys are powered by miniature fusion reactors of their own, and carry hydrogen fuel in tanks below the seating area. They stay aloft by inhaling cool air and superheating it, expelling it below decks in rocket fashion without pro-ducing the lung-clotting exhaust our present-day, gasoline-powered engines do. Atomic power is clean power!

Some people—usually the young—race through town using the public air lanes above the trol-ley lane. They drive personal air-cars shaped like UFOs, smaller than the Chevrolet you have in your garage but ten times as fast. These colorful vehicles can be seen in the skies all across the world, carrying tourists who prefer to travel private-ly or only with loved ones and who don't mind spending the extra time watching the scenery pass below. A typical air-car can cruise at half the speed of sound while consuming less than a pound of hydrogen per hundred miles; only specially armored, commercial cruisers are sturdy enough to withstand the crushing blow that accompanies breaking the sound barrier.

Those who must reach their des-tination as fast as possible can choose from many alternatives, though the costs rise as fast as the desired speed. Anyone can afford to fly aboard a strato-plane, and Captain Proton does just that in order to track the villain to Kansas City. He spends less than six hours in the air and the ride costs him the equivalent of any air ticket. Along the way, he sees the great Midwest Floating Fields. The Fields fill tens of thousands of square miles of sky, glinting with robotic workers; gone are the days of toiling in the mud and wasting beautiful scenery for growing crops! Now the very air itself provides the world with nutrition. Great clouds of foodplants waft through the skies over our heartland, safe from insects and storms, tended and harvested by gentle robots. These farm-clouds actually obstruct the sun less than the typical summer puffballs while providing the same, much-welcomed shade. In fact, water-vapor clouds often form the heart of the Floating Fields, which absorb them. The Fields greatly reduce unwanted rain. Never mind those short-sighted complainers that Captain Proton witnesses at the airport; who really likes to be rained on, anyway?

When Captain Proton realizes his quarry is one step ahead of him and is en route to Hong Kong, he spends about five times as much to ride a jump-rocket. This trip only lasts an hour, but he lands with a sore back from the acceleration. Now the super-villain leads him on an underwater race back to Seattle, and Captain Proton pays double airfare to ride a high-speed, luxury submarine liner which uses ocean water to power its fusion reactor and jet through the hollow center of the doughnut-shaped vessel. This ride lasts eight hours and is a bit rougher than the air trips.

Weapons of the Year 2000

AFTER CAPTAIN PROTON and the super-villain disembark at Pier 104 back in Seattle, the villain's henchmen open fire with handheld atomic ray guns. These are no bigger than the revolvers of our day, but their mini-reactors can unleash power equal to modern-day cannon! Atomic ray guns can also be designed as artillery for use in eliminating machines and buildings, but these use reactors to fire uranium slugs or spray jets of million-degree fire. Of course, such artillery is much larger and restricted to military use.

Captain Proton easily outwits these henchmen using a Solaradium shield to reflect the atomic energies of their ray guns back at those very ray guns, melting them right out of the men's hands. Before they get done dunking their red hands in the water of a multicolored fountain, Captain Proton has them securely fastened to one another with spider cord, a super-light, unbreakable rope he picked up at the submarine gift shop. But their leader has vanished.

Captain Proton picks up the villain's scent . . . and discovers the man has launched into space! Captain Proton must spend ten times a normal airfare to hire a ride to Earth Station Ten aboard a common ground-to-orbit rocket. These atomic-powered craft are shaped like bullets, but bullets that can carry a dozen people—and their fifty pounds of luggage each—to the wheel shaped Earth Stations in less than ten minutes. These four thousand orbiters serve as way stations to the rest of the Solar System, hotels for the wealthy, retirement homes for the frail (who exalt in the low-gravity sections), and scientific laboratories. But, perhaps most important, they house the Earth's Planetary Defenses. Each Station contains one atomic laser powerful enough to instantly melt the largest interplanetary-battleship into slag, as well as several hundred smaller lasers, individually manned, suitable for combating whole fleets of fighters and other small craft. But wait; the magic of year-2000 super-science doesn't stop there! All four thousand Stations can merge their mega-lasers into one huge pulse they call the "Equalizer." No evil world in this Galaxy or any of the other visible galaxies can hide from Earth's defenses! Humanity is forever safe from unwanted aggression of any scale.

Captain Proton Saves the Future

YET CRIMINALS and madmen will always abound, so we will always need men like Captain Proton. Witness this: Shortly after his arrival on Earth Station Ten, he tracks down the super-villain to the heart of the orbiter. There Captain Proton discovers the dead bodies of five brave soldiers whose job it was to operate the mega-laser; they float in zero-gravity, necks broken by the villain's pulse gun that was undetectable to the spaceport authorities. These weapons are very rare anywhere but in the hands of the world military, using an atomic-powered gravity lens to thrust a crushing shockwave from their disklike forward projector. Some— such as the villain's—are small enough to be shaped into a ring yet can capture enough gravity power to break any bone in a man's body.

Captain Proton quietly works his way across an auditorium-sized

room lined with humming atomic generators. At the center of the room stands the mega-laser itself; its synthetic-ruby cylinder is as tall as the Statue of Liberty and as wide as a city bus; and over its controls stands the evil genius, his devious plan about to be executed. Just as the generators start to hum louder, just as a faint glow begins to appear at the core of the giant ruby, Captain Proton seizes the moment to launch himself from a wall across the empty space and capture the villain using magneto-cuffs, inescapable handcuffs of the future.

His job done, Captain Proton brings the villain to Earth Security, where the man will face justice.

After it all, Captain Proton looks out a station porthole upon the Earth's blue sphere rolling through a field of stars, and he recalls the adventures of this day, all the places down there he visited, and marvels at this grand world and all its technology that he takes for granted. This was only one day in an astounding life.

Captain Proton smiles a wise yet wistful smile, knowing that the very super-science that nearly destroyed the world today also saved it. Deranged minds will always fail when confronted by such minds as our hero has, and super-science is only as powerful as the man who wields it!

SCREAM AND SCREAM AGAIN

By Jester Lee

The ray of light came in through the window like a river of warmth, flowing over Constance Goodheart and her perfectly clean desk like high clouds over distant mountain peaks, like the laugh over a lover's lips, like the water of her bath around her body the night before. The light soothed her, made her smile just as her bath had done. She loved baths, she loved warm light. Sometimes the thought of taking a bath in the sunlight made her shiver with pleasure. Often when tied up and threatened by Weapons of Death and Destruction by some evil villain Captain Proton was fighting, she thought of warm baths in the bright sun. The thought often kept her from screaming.

So as the warm ray of light bathed her and her perfectly clean desk, she didn't think of mountain peaks or lover's lips, but instead thought of taking a real bath, and the thought made her shiver as it always did.

She smiled, her eyes closed. Daydreaming was always better with her eyes closed. Captain Proton had told her that once, and since then she had always closed her eyes in her best daydreams. Sometimes she could bring on a really, really good daydream simply by closing her eyes. But she didn't use that power often. But in the warm ray of light, a daydream seemed natural, so she closed her eyes.

It wasn't until the warmth of the light dimmed and the memory of warm water eased into the back of her mind that Constance Goodheart, secretary to Captain Proton, again opened her eyes.

At first she thought she'd been taken to another room, much bigger than her office, with the strangest-looking furniture. But she hadn't felt anything move her. Even the really nifty Move-It-Around-Ray that the people of Voy had invented still had a sensation of tingling when used. She had just been warm, her eyes closed, daydreaming, thinking of a bath. She hadn't felt any tingling, she was sure.

Shivering, maybe, but not tingling.

Now she was sitting on the edge of what looked to be a huge chair, her feet dangling off the ground. She remembered sitting like that when she was a little girl. She had hated it then. She didn't much like it now, either.

Then she realized it was her chair she was sitting on. And her huge desk that seemed to stretch out in front of her like a vast plain of smooth wood, empty and shining. She had a thought: Something had caused her office to get much, much bigger.

Or she had shrunk.

It took her a moment before that second thought sunk completely in. She was proud of her full-sized, robust figure. Her worst nightmare was shrinking.

And the more she thought about shrinking, the more panicked she got.

Finally, it had to happen. Welling up out of her like an exploding volcano, she tipped her head back, took a deep breath, and screamed.

The sound sort of half-echoed around the seemingly huge room. Usually her screams filled all of a space and made people turn. Now her scream was as small as she was and actually didn't fill much of anything, sounding almost hollow in the echo. Had someone put a dreaded scream-dampening-field over her office?

No, she decided. That couldn't be the cause. The scream was small because she was small.

What had happened to her? What had caused the shrinkage? Was she still shrinking?

That thought made her scream again, another pitiful excuse of a sound, and it didn't make her feel even the slightest bit better.

She looked around, gazing out over the top of her desk like peeking over the edge of a window. It had to be her office that was growing.

That was it. The office had grown. An Expando-Ray could do that. It would have taken some time. Maybe her daydream had lasted longer than she had thought. They did that sometimes.

She looked down at herself. Her dress still fit just as it had this morning. Therefore, she couldn't be shrinking. The office had to be growing.

She nodded. She had the answer. But why? And how? Now that she thought about it, Expando-Rays make a loud roaring sound when used. She hadn't heard any roaring sound. So what could have happened to her office, her desk, her chair to make it swell up like this? Was it something she'd done? She'd never had that effect on furniture before.

Maybe it had been the warm beam of light?

But the light coming in the window had only been focused on her, not the entire office. So it couldn't be the entire office. It had to be only her. She was shrinking, dress and all.

With the thought of the comforting bath and swelling furniture now pushed far away, she screamed again.

The sound echoed again, quickly muffled by the seemingly immense size of the room. Why couldn't someone hear her? Often her screams made Captain Proton come running. When the beam of light came though the window, he'd been in his office, doing important Galactic Hero work, getting ready for their next mission. His door was closed. So why couldn't he hear her scream?

She screamed again.

Nothing.

She forced herself to take a deep breath. Captain Proton, her boss, had told her when in a tight spot, always take a deep breath. It cleared the head, made things not seem so bad, he had told her. Actually, it gave her more air for another scream, so she screamed again.

No one came running. The door to Captain Proton's office remained solidly closed. Maybe he had been hit with a warm ray of light and been shrunk, too.

And if that was the case, then he would just now be defeating the bad guy who did the shrinking and would soon come and restore her to her full-sized beauty. He'd saved her a hundred times before, he'd do it again if he just knew she was tiny, too.

As soon as he took care of the bad guy.

She screamed again, really, really loud this time, putting everything she could behind it.

She listened to the echo. Captain Proton did not come running and she couldn't hear any sounds of a fight going on in the other room.

She took another deep breath and this time didn't scream. Captain Proton was right. It did clear her head. Not as well as thoughts of warm baths and bright light, but almost. She was about to jump down from her chair and go to her boss' door, when another thought hit her: What if moving made it worse?

Captain Proton often told her to just stay in one place. When in danger, moving around made things worse. He never had said what the "things" were exactly each time, but she hadn't asked either. What if she jumped down from her chair and shrank some more? That might be a "thing." Then where would she be?

She had been kidnapped by the most evil villains of the Galaxy, tied up in spaceships and castles, threatened to be shot by death rays and poison-tipped darts. Danger and getting tied up was part of the job description working as the secretary for the galaxy's top hero. But never had she been shrunk. Her dress had been shrunk once, but both Captain Proton and Buster Kincaid, ace reporter, swore they had averted their eyes at the appropriate time in the rescue.

But now she was the size of a large baby, dressed in a tight dress, with the shrunken body of a woman. She needed help and she needed it fast. But unless she had no other choice, she would stay put, on her own chair, just to make sure she didn't make "things" worse. Right now she still had another choice.

She screamed again. Really long and loud this time, putting all her small lungs behind it, and aiming the scream as best she could at Captain Proton's office door.

A moment later the door slammed open. "Constance, don't you understand I'm trying to—"

She sort of waved and smiled at him over the top of the desk like a child waving at a parade.

"Oh, no!" Captain Proton shouted. "The Balloon People! They're already here. I didn't expect them from the Cloud System for at least another day."

She wanted to ask him: *What Balloon People?* And if he knew she was going to get shrunk, the least he could have done was warn her.

But she didn't get the chance. At that moment, riding on the warm beam of light, a dozen Balloon People smashed through the window and floated down into the office, scattering like leaves in front of a high wind, ending up in all corners of the room. Constance used to love playing with balloons and in the leaves when she was a child, just about the size she was right now. Except back then it was natural to be this size. Right now she didn't want any balloons or leaves. And she wanted to be bigger.

Each Balloon Person was about the size of a good, overripe melon, had four little legs, two fat arms carrying tiny guns, and an ugly, smiling face indented in the side of the balloon. Some were red, others blue, a few green. The leader of the Balloon People seemed to be the yellow one with the pink ribbon who sneered at her.

She screamed.

"Stay down!" Captain Proton shouted to her, then dove for his office door, rolling on the floor and coming up kneeling, his trusty twin ray guns in both hands.

Down? Down where? What did he mean by that? She was only two feet tall. How much more down could she get? She screamed again and then ducked as Captain Proton started firing.

Pop!

Pop!

Fizz! Fizz!

The Balloon-People were firing back. She hoped Captain Proton could stay out of the way. Those Fizz-weapons didn't sound good.

Pop! Pop!

Fizz! Fizz!

Captain Proton was such a good shot. It was one of the many things she admired about him.

Pop! Pop! Pop!

Seven Balloon People no longer had their air. How many more could there be left?

Fizz! Fizz!

Four Balloon People hovered over her head, pointing weapons at her.

She screamed, expecting to be fizzed at any moment.

Instead, they all sort of floated down beside her and grabbed her with their rubbery-feeling little hands. Then they tried lifting her.

Pop!

They had shrunken her so they could kidnap her!

She screamed again.

Pop! Pop!

Two more Balloon People ran into the point of Captain Proton's ray guns.

The four Balloon People who had their little rubbery paws on her tried to lift.

She screamed.

They didn't budge her. Luckily she'd had a full lunch instead of just a salad.

Suddenly, as if from the land of the giants, Captain Proton loomed over her and the four Balloon People who were trying to lift her.

"Get your hot air off my secretary!" He exclaimed, pointing both ray guns right at the four Balloon People.

They let go of her and started to rise toward the ceiling, trying to draw their Fizz-Guns as they went.

"Drop those weapons! Float

right there!" Captain Proton ordered. "Or join your gas god on the other side of the rubber!"

They stopped and dropped their weapons. One hit Constance on the head and she screamed.

"Reverse your Shrinking Ray!" Captain Proton demanded. Now!"

"Or you'll do what?" the Balloon Person with the ribbon snorted, floating over beside his four remaining Balloon People.

Captain Proton flipped one ray gun into his holster with a twirl, and with his now free hand grabbed the leader of the Balloon People. Quickly he rubbed the Balloon-Leader on his pants leg, up and down, up and down, real fast.

"Ow! Hey, that tickles. Ouch! Not so hard!" the Balloon-Leader shouted.

Then, just as quickly as he had started, Captain Proton stopped rubbing the Balloon-Leader and turned and stuck the Balloon-Leader to the wall.

Instantly Constance knew what her boss had just done. When she was a kid she had rubbed balloons on her dresses and then stuck them to walls. It had always been lots of fun. It must still be fun because Captain Proton was smiling.

"Hey!" Balloon-Leader shouted. "Let me down!" The little guy kicked his feet and waved his hands, but it didn't do any good. He was stuck on the wall right beside the Incorporated Planets symbol.

"Bring my secretary back to normal size and I'll think about it," Proton replied. "Otherwise I'll stick all of you on the wall and dig out my darts. I was the Incorporated Planets dart champion. I never miss."

The four Balloon People who were floating above her seemed to vibrate with that threat. Their little rubbery faces seemed to pucker, as if they were losing air.

Their leader struggled and struggled, but didn't come unstuck. Finally he sighed, "All right, Captain Proton!" The Balloon-Leader pulled out what looked like a lollipop and spoke into it in his native language. *"Hiss-hiss. Hiss-sss-hisss-hisssss."*

Instantly the warm beam of light was focused on her again.

She screamed.

"Hold on Constance!" Captain Proton warned.

His voice calmed her and she tried to relax with the light. But this time she didn't close her eyes.

Slowly, as if she were getting closer to something in the distance, the room around her got smaller and smaller until finally she was sitting normally at her desk. She glanced down at her dress. Luckily it was still perfectly sized. Pieces of rubber littered the office, and small burn marks surrounded Captain Proton's office door from the Great Balloon Gunfight.

Captain Proton reached out and grabbed two of the remaining four Balloon People. "Constance. Get the other two."

He started rubbing them on his legs.

Constance stood and looked at the remaining two Balloon People who had looks of intense fear on their rubbery little faces. Carefully, she reached out and grabbed them, making sure to not poke them with her long fingernails. She didn't want to pop one of them and get Balloon guts on her dress.

"Rub them on your skirt," Captain Proton said. Then he turned and stuck the two he held on the wall beside their boss.

She rubbed the rubbery little Balloon People on her legs.

She wanted to scream, but didn't. She stopped rubbing and handed them, disgusted, to Captain Proton, who quickly gave them a hard rub and stuck them beside their friends. Rubbing balloons as an adult just wasn't as much fun as she had remembered it.

Then, hands on his hips, Captain Proton faced the wall full of Balloon People. "Well, are you ready to negotiate for entry into the Incorporated Planets?"

"We are," the Balloon-People leader said. "You have proven you can beat us. We will gladly join an organization that is more powerful than we are. Safer that way."

"Good," Captain Proton replied, nodding. "I'll get the treaty for you to sign."

He turned and marched back into his office.

Constance watched him go, wishing that someday he would finally get around to asking her to marry him. She sighed and sat down on her chair, staring at the Balloon People on the wall. It had all been a test. Her shrinking had been just part of a big entrance exam for the Balloon People. She

sure wished Captain Proton had warned her. But there must have been a reason that he hadn't. He always had a good reason and it was always right.

"I feel myself slipping," one Balloon Person said.

Constance frowned at the five Balloon People stuck to her office wall.

"Yeah, I'm slipping too," another agreed.

The leader of the Balloon-People looked at her and then winked. "Guess you'd better rub us again."

"Please," another whispered.

At that moment one of them fell off the wall, floating down and toward her, smiling. She jumped back, sliding up on her desk to get away from the evil creature.

It floated toward her.

She backed up, sliding across the top of her desk.

It kept coming.

The only thing she could think to do was scream.

Behind her, in his office door, Captain Proton laughed and the evil Balloon Creature frowned and floated back toward the wall with the others.

Once again Captain Proton had saved her.

A typical day in the life of the secretary of the Galaxy's most famous hero.

THE FORGOTTEN AND LOST RACE

by *Don Simster*

Buster Kincaid glanced around, his sharp ace reporter eye catching every detail, every odd piece of information. He very seldom missed anything when it came to details. And right now, there was a lot to observe. He and his friend, Captain Proton, along with Captain Proton's beautiful secretary, Constance Goodheart, were tied to wooden posts in a clearing in the middle of a massive jungle deep inside a planet covered in ice. A splinter had cut into his hand. A detail, not important, but painful.

Around them fifty members of the Lost Race sat, their breathing sticks making bubbles in what they called their Pool of Life. The Lost Race looked almost human, except for a few important details. First off, they breathed only water. They could move around in the air, but always seemed to have a strawlike hose or stick in water to breathe.

They wore skin-tight suits with different colored circles on them to indicate some sort of rank Kincaid had yet to figure out, even with his sharp eye for details. The Lost Race also had no eyelids and huge black eyes that made it seem as if they were always staring and must have made it really tough for them to go out into bright light. Right now all fifty of them were staring at their three prisoners across the Pool of Life.

Sweat ran down Kincaid's face, back, and arms. The jungle around them was an impossible jungle. They had been on a mission to the ice-covered planet called Red Mountain. The planet had that strange name because of the one red-coned mountain that stuck above the plane of ice that covered the rest of the planet. The desert planet of Phoenix Prime needed water and Captain Proton had volunteered to explore Red Mountain to see if the ice there would help them.

But just after landing, things had gone wrong for them. Constance had slipped into a giant crevice in the ice, and when Captain Proton and Kincaid had lowered themselves down on ropes to save her, they had discovered warm air coming from a vent in the ice at the bottom of the crevice.

Captain Proton had decided they would explore the vent, but halfway down they all slipped and slid down into this huge warm ocean, where the Lost Race people captured them and tied them up in this jungle near what they had called their Pool of Life. All and all, it had not been a good day.

"What are they going to do with us?" Kincaid asked Captain Proton.

Proton only shrugged against his bonds. "I don't think it will be anything good for our health. But I'm still struck by how human they look. Does that seem odd to you?"

"I think getting killed by them down here in this jungle under all this ice is odd," Kincaid replied. "I don't have any idea what to think of them. Why did you call them the Lost Race when we were captured?"

Captain Proton shrugged. "I read an old book once where humanlike creatures were living underground. In the book they were called the Lost Race."

"As good a name as any, I suppose," Kincaid replied.

Captain Proton only nodded sagely. Kincaid knew that when Proton did that, he was going deep in thought and shouldn't be disturbed.

Constance sobbed, slumped against her post. She had stopped screaming ten minutes ago. Kincaid figured she had just worn herself out. Captain Proton never seemed to notice her screaming, for some reason. Kincaid grew tired of it quickly, but had never said a word. At least not yet. Maybe someday he would.

Kincaid tried to work against the ropes holding him, but only managed to shove the splinter deeper into his arm. He just hoped he would live long enough to worry about getting that splinter out and asking Constance to stop screaming so much.

"It seems things are changing," Captain Proton said softly as all fifty of the Lost Race stood as one, the spots on their body suits making it a very odd sight.

"When they untie us," Captain Proton whispered, "I'll create a diversion. I want you two to run, get back to the surface and the ship, go for help."

"But Captain," Kincaid objected. "We'll never make it back with help before they kill you!"

"A chance I'll have to take," Captain Proton replied, stiffening his shoulders as two of the Lost Race moved to each pole and began to untie them.

Captain Proton waited until it was clear that they were all untied, then he lurched against his two captors, knocking them both into the Pool of Life with a mighty shove.

Kincaid instantly smashed his boot down on the bare foot of one of his captors. It hopped away making yipping noises through its breathing straw, blowing huge bubbles in the Pool of Life.

Captain Proton punched out the two holding Constance, then quickly dove at the last one still grasping Kincaid. Kincaid felt his arm yank as the creature was torn away by Captain Proton's forceful blow.

"Run!" Proton shouted, turning to face the onrushing hound of Lost Race creatures, moving around the pool at them while keeping their breathing sticks in the water.

Kincaid turned and started to dash toward the jungle, away from the pool, when he heard Constance scream.

He stopped and looked back. The Lost Race people had covered Captain Proton in a mass of bodies, but Kincaid could tell he was still fighting. Constance had been grabbed by the guard with the hurt

foot and two others were running toward her.

Kincaid knew that if he went back to help her, he too would be captured and all of Captain Proton's valiant fighting would be wasted. He had to follow Captain Proton's orders and escape. It was the only chance they all had.

He turned and headed for the jungle at full speed, moving up hill as much as he could. He figured the closer he got to the ice walls and ceiling of this huge underground jungle, the less chance any of them would follow him.

Behind him he heard Constance scream once more, then the sounds were muffled as he ducked into the thick brush.

Captain Proton had once told him that the best way to avoid someone chasing you is to do exactly the opposite of what they would expect you to do. Right now, Kincaid knew the Lost Race creatures would expect him to keep running away from the Pool of Life, toward the ice. He had to do something different at first, to throw them off track. Ten paces into the jungle he turned right, moving along the edge of the jungle, going around the clearing and the Pool of Life.

After about a hundred running steps he stopped and ducked behind a log, trying to calm his heavy breathing so he could hear if someone was close behind him.

Nothing.

He waited.

Nothing.

No one was chasing him. Was it possible they couldn't move very far from the water? Was getting away really that easy?

He waited another full minute before easing up from his hiding place. Then cautiously, he moved toward the edge of the clearing, checking every detail before each step to make sure he made no noise. Finally he was behind a large tree where he could see the clearing and the Pool of Life. Captain Proton and Constance were being led around the Pool  of Life. They both seemed to be all right, which was a great relief to Kincaid.

On the other side, the Lost Race creatures stopped and formed a line along the Pool of Life. One creature touched a pole sticking in the ground, then looked upward and shouted, "Ancestors, hear us!"

Then to Kincaid's astonishment, the ground near the pool started to open.

Slowly, the rumble filled the air as the rocks moved back, forming a round hole.

Constance screamed over the sound, but it seemed to Kincaid more like a faint squeak.

"The Pit That Time Forgot," one creature shouted when the rumbling stopped.

The other creatures hooted and blew in their breathing tubes, forming huge bubbles in the Pool of Life.

The lead creature stopped them

after a moment and faced Captain Proton. "Intruders in our world, you who dared to swim in the Sea of Living, connected to the Pool of Life, you are sentenced to spend two units of time in the Pit That Time Forgot."

"Exactly how long is two units?" Kincaid heard Captain Proton ask, his voice level.

"For you," the leader answered, "it will seem as only a moment."

Kincaid noticed the wrong sounding detail in the sentence, the two words that were the most frightening. "For you . . ."

"I assume," Proton pushed, noticing the same two words that Kincaid had noticed, "that time will be longer outside the Pit."

"My great, great, great grand-child will be the one to greet you when you come out."

"And we will be free to go at that time," Proton asked.

"Of course," the leader said. "You violated our home, contaminated the very water that sustains us. This is your punishment."

Kincaid wanted to run into the clearing and shout, "No!" But instead he remained frozen behind the tree, making no sound as Captain Proton nodded to the leader of the Lost Race, then took Contance's arm and stepped down into the Pit. Clearly there must be some sort of staircase there.

Down, down, down, as if the Pit were slowly swallowing them feet-first.

After they vanished, the Pit slowly closed back up with more massive rumbling. Then all of the creatures dropped their breathing tubes and simply dove back into the Pool of Life, vanishing under the surface. They didn't even leave a guard.

Kincaid stayed silent, watching the clearing, waiting.

Nothing moved.

In the giant cave under the ice there was no wind. Just heat and jungle and the clearing with the Pool of Life that lead to the vast ocean they had fallen into after sliding down the vent in the ice.

Finally, after waiting a good hour, Kincaid stood and moved slowly back into the meadow, expecting a Lost Race creature to appear out of the Pool of Life at any moment.

None did.

Kincaid moved up to the post the leader of the Lost Race creatures had touched to get the Pit to open. It looked just like any other post stuck in the rock. Wooden, worn in a number of places, rounded on the top.

He touched it, then waited for the ground to open.

Nothing.

He shoved the post.

Nothing.

He inspected the post, looking for buttons or levers.

Nothing.

"Okay," he said to himself. "Think."

In his mind he went over what the leader of the Lost Race creatures had done to open the hole in the rock. Detail by detail. He was just about to repeat every tiny move when the clearing was filled with a low growling.

Kincaid looked around, then froze. Coming out of the jungle on one side of the clearing were three massive dog-like creatures. They had red eyes, long, sharp teeth, and saliva dipping and foaming around their mouths. Their shoulders were as tall as he was. Never in all his life had he seen such huge canine creatures.

Kincaid knew without a doubt that if those hounds caught him, he would be their next meal. Actually, at their size, he would be just a snack. Running faster than he had run in a long time, he turned and headed across the clearing into the jungle.

The hounds were behind him, chasing him. But the good news was they weren't gaining ground on him. The bad news was that he wasn't gaining any ground on them either.

Focusing on the path ahead through the jungle, making sure of every step so that he didn't trip, he ran for the ice. Behind him the three hounds crashed through the brush. Kincaid had no doubt that as big as they were, they were just running right through the small trees.

The ground sloped upward in front of him and the jungle was getting thinner. But he was also getting tired. He didn't dare even slow down.

The higher he climbed, the thinner the jungle, until finally he broke out onto a rock slope that slanted up toward a huge ice wall. It was much cooler up here, which felt good to his sweating, exhausted body.

He allowed himself to look back. The giant hounds were still coming. Ahead of him he just hoped there was an opening in the ice wall, or he was going to be trapped there, a cold snack for the hounds.

A few minutes later he had reached the wall and turned to the right, running and scrambling along the ice where it met the rock. It was hard going for him, but behind him the hounds were having the same problem.

Finally, when it seemed as if there was no hope, he came upon a massive crack in the ice. A small stream ran out of the crack and down toward the jungle. He forced himself to stop for just an instant. If this crack lead to the surface, there would be a breeze blowing through it. Did he feel a breeze?

He tried to stand still as behind him the hounds gained ground, growling, dripping saliva. If he didn't hurry, they would soon be dripping his blood out of their mouths.

Yes! There was a breeze, blowing into the crack. There was a way out here.

He sprang back into motion, at first running up the rock slope inside the crack, then slowing as the crack narrowed.

Finally, the crack narrowed so much that he could barely slip through. He knew the hounds behind him would never fit. He was safe at least for the moment.

He stopped, working to catch his breath as he watched the growling hounds try to force their broad shoulders up into the crevice and fail.

"Sorry guys," he said aloud. "You'll have to find another dinner today."

One of them looked at him with glaring red eyes and Kincaid shuddered. It was time to move on. He had to get back to the ship, get some weapons and equipment and come back and rescue Captain Proton and Constance from the Pit That Time Forgot.

It took him the rest of the day to get up through the ice to the surface and another few hours to find the ship.

The first thing he did was make himself a good meal and warm up, then he started putting together the equipment he would need to go back. He worked slowly and carefully, finally falling asleep only after everything was ready. Even though he knew Captain Proton and Constance wouldn't be noticing the time passing in the Pit That Time Forgot, he still slept fitfully, as if not going back at once was wrong. Would Captain Proton have gone back at once? Or would he have rested first, made sure he was ready? Kincaid didn't know and made a mental note to ask Proton after he was rescued.

Ten hours later, well fed and rested, he started back for the crack in the ice that lead down into the clearing and the Pool of Life. He was carrying three weapons, blasting equipment in case he had to go through the rock to get them out, and food. It was a heavy load, which made the going slow, but he

managed, only slipping a few times getting back down the ice crevice.

Eight hours later he inched through the jungle, Energy Ray Gun ready and armed in case any monster hounds appeared, until finally he was on the edge of the clearing that contained the Pool of Life. It had now been a full two days since Captain Proton and Constance had gone down into the Pit That Time Forgot. Kincaid just hoped the Lost Race leader had been right and it would only seem like a moment to Captain Proton and Constance. Otherwise they were going to be really hungry and thirsty by the time he got them out of there.

He was just about to head out into the clearing when the heads of Lost Race creatures appeared in the Pool of Life and slowly climbed out, picking up breathing sticks and putting one end back in the water.

Fifty of them lined up again along the edge of the Pool, then one of them moved forward, touched the pole stuck in the ground and said, "Ancestors, hear me." Again a massive rumbling shook the ground as the earth opened into the Pit That Time Forgot.

Kincaid couldn't figure out what was going on. Did the Lost Race creatures have someone else to put down there? Kincaid couldn't see anyone if they did.

Maybe they had had a change of heart and were letting Captain Proton and Constance out. Could that be possible? Or maybe they had decided to kill them instead. But either way, now was his chance.

The Pit was open, he had weapons. It was time for a rescue.

He put the food down, took a second ray gun for his left hand, then jumped up and ran into the clearing, ray guns in both hands.

"Don't anyone move!" he shouted.

As if on one neck, every head of every Lost Race creature turned and looked at him, the lidless eyes staring at him like he was something completely unexpected.

"Now let them out of the Pit!" Kincaid ordered, moving up so that he faced the Lost Race creatures. He kept both ray guns aimed at the leader near the pole, in case he moved to close up the Pit and trap Captain Proton and Constance.

"No need for that, my friend," Captain Proton said from the Pit as he helped Constance up the steep steps just inside the rock hole. "We have served our term.  We are free to go. Is that correct?"

The leader of the Lost Race nodded. "You have served your time. You are free to leave now, as was ordered by my great, great, great grandfather, in the time before yesterday."

Kincaid lowered his weapons as Captain Proton smiled at him. In all his years he had never been so confused. "How? Why?"

Captain Proton laughed. "I'll explain it all when we get back to the ship. And from the looks of your equipment, you know the way."

Kincaid could only nod.

Captain Proton turned to face the leader of the Lost Race. "We are sorry we broke your laws, swam in your Sea of Living. It will not happen again."

The leader bowed slightly to Captain Proton, who returned the bow, always the perfect diplomat. Then Captain Proton took Constance's arm and lead her to where Kincaid waited.

"Time to get out of here," Proton exclaimed.

"And not a minute too soon for me," Kincaid said, as he turned and headed back for the jungle, keeping a sharp eye out for monster hounds.

Back in the ship, as the Red Mountain ice planet vanished in the distance behind them, Kincaid turned to Captain Proton. "You knew all along you were only going to be in that Pit for a few days."

"Of course," Proton laughed. "Give or take a day or so. Otherwise I would have fought to stay out of it."

"But how did you know?"

"Details, my dear friend," Captain Proton answered. "During the time we were being held, the leader aged dramatically. He was young when we were captured, almost an old man when I faced him near the Pit. When he told me of our sentence, I knew it would not be for long."

"So the Lost Race age very quickly," Kincaid said.

"Twelve hours is a long life, I would guess," Proton said. "And since under the ice, in the oceans, there is no such thing as day or night, their life spans seem normal to them."

"And time didn't stand still for you in the Pit?" Kincaid asked.

Captain Proton quickly steered their ship around an Asteroid Shower, then shook his head. "We slept, mostly. Luckily I had a few rations and there was water in the Pit to drink, or we would have been very hungry. But it turned out almost pleasant, didn't it Constance."

Constance almost nodded.

Kincaid laughed. "Glad it turned out the way it did. Can't believe I didn't see the detail of them aging. I'm supposed to see details."

"Not something you would normally look for," Proton said. "And by the way, thank you for the rescue attempt."

Kincaid smiled. It wasn't often that Captain Proton thanked anyone for anything. Usually people were thanking him for saving them. "You are more than welcome."

"So," Proton continued, "tell us about your two days outside the Pit. Was it eventful?"

"Very," Kincaid answered. And then set off telling them how he escaped. In the telling, the ice got slicker, the cold colder, the hounds bigger and closer in the chase. But  all that didn't matter. It was just details. He got all the big stuff right, just as any good reporter would do.

A few words before we blast off on our regularly scheduled flight to other worlds. I've been getting a lot of letters by readers who care about where our kind of fiction is going, and I've decided that'll take a lot more talking than usual.

It's time for you readers to pick up the charge. Write me, and attend scientifiction conventions, and get new readers involved in scientifiction!

As we journey through the twentieth century, where do you think scientifiction is going? Where do you want to steer the great rocketship of the genre?

Read on, Ensigns!

WHAT A MESS!
by Leonard R. Findleson

DEAR SARGE:

I variciously enjoy anticipating the arrival of your fiction periodical, and often that enjoyment is matched by the quality of story populating the space between the lurid covers. Which reminds me, the cover art you consigned for Vol. 3, No. 2 was exceptionally inappropriate for the content of the issue. Although the story "Captain Proton and the Sandmen of Mercury" involved a female heroine who assisted the grand Captain in his mission, at no time did either of them wear clothing in the least reminiscent of the cover art (which was clearly supposed to illustrate this story; it is obvious to anyone, considering how large the Sun is against the crystalline surface of the planet). Anyone "in the know" is aware that a human walking around in a bathing suit on the surface of the planet Mercury (mean distance from Sun: 36,000 miles; equatorial diameter: 3000 miles) would die instantly!

That aside, I wish to express my enjoyment of the story by Robert F. Danman, entitled, "Captain Proton and the Caverns of Doom." I especially enjoyed the loquacity of the Captain when he extricated himself from the rostrum of the evil Lord Dragoon during the river battle aboard the vicariant vessel, "Drum." He is so cavalierly cartesiatic!

Then I began to be distracted by typographical errors you and your editorial assistants should have easily spotted and corrected. For example, on page 126, the text reads, "Captain Proton donned his blaster belt and he leaped from the rail of his schooner to the planks of Lord Dragoon's vessel, knocking aside two pirates before even drawing the weapon." Anyone with a basic education in the English language comprehends that one doesn't merge two unrelated clauses in such a way. You must use a comma before the conjuncture, in this case, "and." However, my editorial suggestion is that such sentences be better utilized if split into two discretionary sentences instead of trying to keep them as one.

I will not go into every instance of misappropriation of the English language that I identified on the pages of your magazine, but let it be said by me that you truly need to keep a diasporic eye clearly focused on the quality of language you publish, otherwise educated readers (myself included) will continually be disinclined to continue subscribing, and, instead go in search of finer-edited fiction.

I couldn't've said it better myself, Ensign Findlehammer! I'll crack my whip harder behind my editorial assistant(s!) from now on. By the way, for more about the mysterious planet Mercury, see The Planets of the Future, *elsewhere in this issue.*

THE IMPORTANCE OF ACCURATE SCIENCE
by Dirk Renschenhammer, a.k.a. "Dr. Dirk"

DEAR "SARGE":

Being a fan of your magazine who works at a prestigious Eastern Technological University, I feel it is my duty to point out some scientific shortfalls in the fine stories you have published.

For example, in "Alien Invasion Foiled Again!" by Jack "Doctor" Michaelson, we see this sentence:

"As Captain Proton stood firmly on the smoky, flickering command bridge of the limping battle cruiser, watching his gunners suddenly open fire on the flagship of the enemy's galactic-conquering fleet, he could hear the distant rumble of that vessel's explosion as it lit up the cluttered asteroid belt with a flash of multichromatic light."

Now, an educated reader cringes whenever he hears mention of sound traveling across vacuum. Physics and chemistry both dictate that sound cannot travel through a vacuum, at least not in the wavelengths that the human ear can observe. I'm certain that I'm not the only reader who cringed at this error. Here is another example from the same story:

"Shaking madly, Captain Proton's still-damaged cruiser accelerated through the speed of light and kept accelerating! The vast pinwheel of stars crowding the endless galaxy whooshed past, leaving behind them rainbow-colored streaks in the velvety blackness of infinite, interstellar space."

Here we find a number of scientific errors. First, everyone knows the speed of light is the upper limit to how fast a spaceship can travel. Look at what Einstein wrote and you will see that, although to outside observers a near-lightspeed vessel might appear to be traveling faster than light, it in fact is not. That's Relativity. Second, the galaxy is not endless; it contains approximately 10 million stars. Third, stars do not leave "rainbow-colored streaks" as a near-lightspeed vessel passes them; in fact, you will not notice much movement at all, because you are not moving faster than the speed of light, and stars are usually hundreds of light-years apart, so you would only notice movement after a few years' travel.

However, artifacts of the Doppler Effect might play a minor part in making approaching stars look "blue," and stars moving away look "red." Fourth, interstellar space is not "infinite." The newest studies anyone can read in the scientific journals point out that the Universe is only four billion years old, and then there's the Relativity Effect, which puts an upper limit on the size of the Universe. It's all very scientific and difficult for the layman to understand, but if your readers are interested, they can check out the scientific journals. Also, the cruiser would not "Shak[e] madly," because there's no air in vacuum, so the waves (similar to those that occur from breaking through the sound barrier) from breaking through the "light barrier" (if there were such a thing, which there is not) would not occur.

I could go on citing other examples from the text of your magazine, but you get the idea. Since I study all the papers that I type for the Professors in the Physics Department at my prestigious Eastern Technological University, I am perhaps more well-versed in the most modern technological knowledge than your average reader or copyeditor. I am willing to go over your manuscripts for scientific accuracy before you send them off to production, and I will do it for a very low fee.

Besides these minor, scientific problems, keep publishing rousing, technologically accurate scientifiction! Oh, and please print more nonfiction articles about future technology and astronomy; those sections are my favorite part of the magazine.

Well, thanks for the offer, "Dr. Dirk," but my editing budget's all tapped out. Just so all you sci-smart Airmen out there don't cringe while reading the stuff on these pages, I'll make sure my assistant reads more of those journals to keep up on modern super-science! And don't worry, science fans. We'll have nonfiction articles every issue—if you keep wantin' 'em!

MORE FIGHTIN'!

by Joe Monty

DEAR SARGE:

Boy do I love reading about Captain Proton and his adventures in outer space! The story by Jack Jackson, "Captain Proton Versus the Moon Men," that was great! And I couldn't put down the magazine during "Captain Proton's Adventure at Alpha Centauri," the mini-novel where he and his loyal companions had to stop the invasion of Earth without firing a weapon on the Centaurian homeworld because they have laws against that. Captain Proton is a genius, plain and true. Who else would have thought to use a paper clip and six jars of alien baby food like that? These kinds of stories are what get me to read instead of just going to sleep after a hard day at the plant.

But then I got to "Baby Turns Six," the touchy-feely yarn by Theodore Salmon. What were you thinking when you picked that one out of the slush pile? Sarge, that wasn't scientifiction, it was about talking and weirdoes and emotions and girl stuff. It wasn't even a Captain Proton story! Heck, I didn't even understand it. Scientifiction isn't about psychology—that's not science! If I wanted to read something like the "Baby" story, I'd pick up *Aunt Martha's Book of Confusion and Depression*. Gee whiz, Sarge! Did you do it just to make grown men cry? That's not why we buy *Captain Proton*. We buy your pulp because it's the only kind of reading we do. If you publish a story like "Baby" again, I swear I'll cancel my subscription for a full year, and I'll tell all my buddies to do the same.

Here's a simple checklist to help you pick the right story: Is Captain Proton the main character? Does the Captain get into lots of fights? Does he get taken prisoner and escape using his wits and high-tech gadgets? Is there an evil villain who must be stopped? Does the fate of the world hang in the balance? Does the reader rocket to strange and wonderful new worlds and meet alien races? Are there lots of super-science machines and weapons?

You usually do such a good job picking Captain Proton stories. Every once in a while, though, you go and publish one of those original stories that none of us guys like to read. Just stop doing that and you'll keep your loyal readers subscribing well into the future.

Thanks for writing, Airman Monty. Boy, would it be exciting to put you and the next reader in the same room for a night! (By the way, if you get ten of your buddies at the

THE RUINATION
OF SCIENTIFICTION

by Norma Rinspad

DEAR EDITOR:

Ijust finished reading my first copy of *Captain Proton,* and I must say I am appalled. Is this the sort of material we want the children—the adult readers of tomorrow—reading? Unfortunately, such dreck as what you print in your magazine tempts (I will not even begin to discuss the cover!) the young and ignorant reader into buying yours over a respectable magazine like *Astounding.* Imagine this horrifying possibility: *Captain Proton* pushes *Astounding* off the racks!

This is unacceptable, yet here is the nightmare I foresee: First, magazines like *Captain Proton* pander to the young and uneducated. Second, kids start telling their friends that the only "hip" magazine is *Captain Proton.* Third, new readership of "real" scientifiction magazines falls. Fourth, advertisers pull their ads from the real magazines and invest more heavily in rags such as *Captain Proton.* Fifth, no real scientifiction is available for new or veteran readers, so the only people who read in our genre are innocents and youths. Sixth, the death knell: The only scientifiction that gets published is drivel, such as that published in your pages.

True, you had the good sense to publish the beautiful and moving tale "Baby Turns Six," by Salmon, but you are allowing children and childish readers to push your magazine into oblivion. If scientifiction as a healthy and evolving genre dies, you'd better believe it will take *Captain Proton* with it.

It has taken many years for people to start taking scientifiction seriously, if even a little bit so. Let us not allow mindless space opera to displace true scientifiction. Let us not allow the literature of the mind to wither and die.

You, Editor, hold in your hands the very future of scientifiction. Much as the man who controls power over the atom must decide if he will use the fruit of his mind for good over evil, you, too, must decide if your creation will work to help build this great genre or demolish it.

I will pick up another copy of *Captain Proton* six months hence (I understand the difficulties of producing a magazine). If I find in your pages more work of Salmon's quality, I will tell all my fellow scientifiction fans and writers to subscribe to your magazine. If, on the other hand, I see only more of the drivel that populates the majority of your pages, I will ensure that none of my friends or colleagues—or their friends, family, or colleagues—ever spend a cent on your magazine, as consumers or advertisers.

It's your choice. Don't blow it.

CAPTAIN PROTON'S FUTURE

by Benny Russell

DEAR SARGE:

A lot of my friends at school make fun of me for reading Captain Proton because they say that adventures like the ones the Captain has could never happen. They're wrong! Captain Proton fights for the good and the right and fairness to everyone. He's showing us how to make our own world better while he fights to save us from bad guys like Dr. Chaotica who think that only their kind should be in charge.

I've been writing my own Captain Proton stories. I haven't told my friends that because they'd just laugh at me. But I know that Captain Proton's future will some-day come true or at least a future a lot like it.

"Onward and Upward!" as Captain Proton might say.

Well, well, well! Whaddya think of that, kind readers? Would you rather see more of the brave Captain, as Airman Monty asks— no, demands! Or do you agree with Ensignette Rinspad, that stories about the Captain are wrecking sci-entifiction? Heck, I'll do whatever you subscribers want . . . our boys are "over there" fighting for democracy, aren't they? So I'm giving you all the vote!

Yep, you guessed it: These last two are the letters that decided me to ask you Readers to tell us where to go. Every current subscriber who sends in a vote automatically be-comes an Airman; everyone who starts a new subscription by sending in this form earns the rank of Ensign—but don't worry, you'll get to be an Airman soon enough! You can earn higher ranks in other ways that you'll learn about in your mem-bership packet.

So keep reading and writing.

ABOUT THE AUTHOR

D.W. "Prof" Smith sold his first short story, "The Dingbats of the Tree People," in 1927 and has been writing science fiction ever since, penning such classics as "Skudove Frenchie" among others. Since turn-ing his attention to writing full-time, he has become one of America's most beloved and fastest authors, writing master works under many names, including Lester Lee, Don Simster, Dean Wesley Smith, and Ray Hamil. He is even rumored to be part of the famous writing team of Sandy and Schofield. Lately he has been writing "The Adventures of Captain Proton," a task the "Prof" says he loves almost more than eating.